The Tales of Belkin

The Tales of Belkin

Alexander Pushkin

Translated by Hugh Aplin

ET REMOTISSIMA PROPE

Hesperus Classics

Hesperus Classics
Published by Hesperus Press Limited
4 Rickett Street, London sw6 1ru
www.hesperuspress.com

First published in Russian, 1831
First published by Hesperus Press Limited, 2009

Introduction and English language translation © Hugh Aplin, 2009
Foreword © Adam Thirlwell, 2009

Designed and typeset by Fraser Muggeridge studio
Printed in Jordan by Al-Khayyam Printing Press

ISBN: 978-184391-185-2

CONTENTS

FOREWORD

1

Let's pretend, for a moment, that the reader doesn't know what's going on.

There the reader is, then, happy and eager, in St Petersburg in 1831 – unimpressed by the Russian nation's prose. A discerning Russian reader who wants prose reads in French. Perhaps, like the late Ivan Petrovich Belkin – the author of the book in your hands – this reader likes dropping in on 'a humble little confectioner's' to 'read the literary journals over a cup of chocolate'. And so this assiduous reader might pick up a volume, advertised as *The Tales of the Late Ivan Petrovich Belkin*. The book contains five stories, with a note 'From the Publisher', signed 'A.P.'. In this note, A.P. quotes at length from a letter containing biographical information about Belkin, written by a man who says he is a neighbour of Belkin's – a neighbour who wishes to remain anonymous. The neighbour informs the publisher that the stories 'are, as Ivan Petrovich used to say, for the most part true, and were heard by him from various persons'. And a footnote by the editor, A.P., names these further narrators:

'The Postmaster' was told to him by Titular Councillor A.G.N., 'The Shot' by Lieutenant-Colonel I.L.P., 'The Undertaker' by the merchant's assistant B.V., 'The Blizzard' and 'Mistress Peasant' by Miss K.I.T.'

What a list of disavowal!

There is the true author of these stories, Alexander Pushkin. And then there is the supposed author, Ivan Petrovich Belkin. There is the editor, A.P., who, one supposes, must be Pushkin himself. And then there are the stories' real authors, hidden behind those initials – A.G.N., and I.L.P., and B.V., and Miss K.I.T.

But at this point, therefore, the cleverer reader in St Petersburg would be able to identify these stories' subjects: their larger meaning. They are about how anyone comes to tell a story about anything at all. They are all examples of second-hand literature. For why else would A.P., the editor of these stories, be so assiduous in quoting Belkin's anonymous neighbour, who stressed that the names of the hamlets and villages in the stories are borrowed from the neighbourhood – 'not through some ill intention, but solely through a lack of imagination'?

To the present reader, in Bamako, or Beijing, or London, who might expect Russian fiction from the nineteenth century to be heavy with philosophy, freighted with theology, these stories will therefore come as a delightful act of lightening: an altruistic form of weightlifting.

2

Alexander Pushkin wrote these stories in the autumn of 1830, on his estate at Boldino. In a productive three months, he wrote four plays, a comic narrative poem, and some lyric poems. More importantly, he also wrote, again in the persona of Belkin, 'The History of the Village of Goryukhino', as well as the final chapter of his novel in verse, *Eugene Onegin*, and, on 26th October, a biographical-fictional fragment.

The bulk of this fragment is a description of a poet, an acquaintance of the writer. It advertises the fact that, like the anonymous neighbour's letter to the editor of Belkin's stories, it is a preface to what will come. But then there is a break: and there follows this broken off paragraph:

'This fragment probably comprised the foreword to a tale which was not written or was lost. – We did not want to destroy it...'

The central question of Pushkin's work at the time, in the autumn of 1830 in Boldino, including his great novel in verse *Eugene Onegin*, was an investigation of the conditions of fiction. Pushkin's emphasis on the foreword was a way of dramatising a central intuition: that most people are limited in the kind of stories they can tell. And so, by contrast, the new kind of novelist envisaged by Pushkin will be the opposite: a storyteller who is not limited in the styles he can choose.

And so these stories by the ineffectual imaginary novelist Ivan Petrovich Belkin are the necessary accompanying experiments to

Pushkin's novel in verse *Eugene Onegin*, a novel which pretends to be a true story about Eugene Onegin, one of Pushkin's friends. In that novel, therefore, he no longer needed a preface, because there he had gone even further: the editorial voice of A.P. had become the narrative voice itself: and yet it was still fictional.

And this was Pushkin's crucial realisation, his radical act of lightening: everything can be treated as fiction. All it needs is the right preface – all it needs is a narrator. And every narrator, even Pushkin, is imaginary, in some way.

Just as later Jorge Luis Borges (who himself wrote a book of prefaces) also blurred the boundaries between the essayistic and the fictional, in his stories which seemed to be prefaces to books which never existed, or which, according to Borges, had been lost. So that rather than fiction being treated as real, the real could always be read as if structured by the conventions of fiction.

3

These tales, then, are parodies, an anthology of narrative cliché.

At this point, perhaps I should register an argument.

Some people dislike parody: they think it is dry and slightly arid, they think it is academic. But parody is not always arid; it can also be a necessary, fruitful thing.

Parody begins as soon as a writer realises that everything, in the end, comes down to style. In the effort of inventing a style, a writer can therefore have fun doodling, mimicking and thus ironising the styles of other writing. It is a form of self-liberation.

It is not therefore accurate to class parody as always dry and aggressive. Parody is at the centre of the novel as an art. For parody is close to quotation. And the development of the novel is the development of various techniques – parody, first-person narration, dialogue, style indirect *libre*. All of these are techniques of quotation.

Many years later, in exile from Russia in Prague, the Russian linguist Roman Jakobson would write an essay called 'Linguistics and Poetics', and he would write that:

'Virtually any poetic message is a quasi-quoted discourse with all those peculiar, intricate problems which 'speech within speech' offers to the linguist. The supremacy of the poetic function over the referential function does not obliterate the reference but makes it ambiguous...'

This insight is the more rarefied abstraction of Pushkin's joyous games in *The Tales of Belkin*. In Pushkin, parody is the basis of his style, and of his theory of fiction – his idea that you cannot just be yourself; you cannot invent a megalomaniac style. You have to, instead, be aware of the styles of others.

Which creates some of the most efficiently comic and ironic short stories ever written: elegant contraptions for the investigation of chance, which close on what Anna Akhmatova called their 'toy-like denouements'.

4

For instance. This is the story: 'The Blizzard'.

Maria Gavrilovna is the daughter of a rich landowner, and in love with Vladimir, a young soldier. Elopement is suggested; romantic Maria agrees. 'Maria Gavrilovna had been raised on French novels, and consequently was in love.' On the agreed night, Maria is driven to the nearby village of Zhadrino, to be married in the church. But then there is a snowstorm, and so the plot develops.

This story is a parody. The plot of the story is schlock; it is all sentiment and artifice and unreality. But there are narrative moments of withdrawal, to signal the artifice. There is the lovely sentence already quoted – with its romanticised logic: 'Maria Gavrilovna had been brought up on French novels, and consequently was in love.' There is the fittingness of the setting for a proposal, where the heroine is found 'by the pond, under a weeping willow, with a book in her hands and in a white dress, like a true heroine of a novel'. A true heroine, of course, would not be compared to a true heroine, in a true novel.

Pushkin's technique throughout these stories is to create mute conversations between thematic details. So that gradually the reader will discover similarities, structural echoes. 'The Blizzard', for instance, will find its echo in the collection's final story, 'Mistress Peasant', another story which involves a marriage based on a deception.

And this structural similarity shows how far Pushkin's analysis of fiction depends on his emphasis on the coincidence. In Pushkin's fiction, he discovers a central truth: a story must involve a coincidence. For a coincidence is simply the zenith of timing.

This, say, is the meaning of the collection's first story: 'The Shot'. The apparent story is simple: a man seeks revenge in a duel – after his opponent, having missed, has been utterly nonchalant in the face of death: he has been absolutely disrespectful. So that the man refuses to shoot, and reserves the right to his shot at any point he likes in the future. It seems like a banal story about honour. But the real story is in the surrounding frame: which is a story of a coincidence. The narrator, on two separate occasions, was given, quite coincidentally, the two halves of the story by each of its protagonists. Which is why the story can now be told.

5

This investigation of chance, however, with the plots' experiments with timing, has a corresponding effect on the reader: suspense.

In the story of Maria Gavrilovna, there is this succession of paragraphs:

The cocks were crowing and it was already light when they reached Zhadrino. The church was locked. Vladimir paid his guide and drove to the priest's yard. His troika was not in the yard. What news awaited him!

But let us return to the good Nenaradovo landowners and see what is going on there.

Not a thing.

And so the narrative continues, with this gap in the story unexplained.

This technique of fake suspense in 'The Blizzard', of deliberately manipulated and exposed suspense, is borrowed from Laurence

Sterne's novel *The Life and Opinions of Tristram Shandy* – a novel that Pushkin adored. In Sterne's novel, the easy technique of creating suspense through omission is present from the very first paragraph.

> *Pray, my dear*, quoth my mother, *have you not forgot to wind up the clock?* *Good G–!* cried my father, making an exclamation, but taking care to moderate his voice at the same time, – *Did ever woman, since the creation of the world, interrupt a man with such a silly question?* Pray, what was your father saying? – Nothing.

He was saying nothing, obviously, because he was engaged in another bedroom pastime entirely.

In Sterne, this interest in advertising lacunae and gaps is there to show how facile is the device of creating the reader's incomprehension. It is an ironisation of the fiction that fiction is not fiction.

And Pushkin delights in gaps too. But his purpose, I think, is more delicate. For just as there are gaps in the plots of *The Tales of Belkin*, there are also more ostentatious gaps in his novel in verse, *Eugene Onegin*. Some of these gaps are deliberate, in that they are simply cuts, which Pushkin decided to retain in the published version. But others are inventions, fake gaps representing non-existent cuts. They are there to blur the boundary between what is real and what is fictional.

And so Vladimir Nabokov, editing Pushkin's novel *Eugene Onegin*, can add his own editorial comment:

> 'It is not unthinkable that this gap is a fictional one, with some musical value – the artifice of a wistful pause, the imitation of a missed heartbeat, the mirage of an emotional horizon, false asterisks of false suspense.'

That suspense is false, however, doesn't mean it isn't moving. And this is Pushkin's invention in his stories, in the autumn of 1830, when he changed the art of Russian fiction – or, let's be more precise, the art of fiction – forever.

– Adam Thirlwell, 2009

INTRODUCTION

Alexander Pushkin wrote *The Tales of Belkin* in a very short time in the autumn of 1830 while staying on one of his family's estates at the village of Boldino. Almost on the eve of his marriage, he was held there for considerably longer than planned by a serious outbreak of cholera in the area, which led to the establishment of a strict quarantine. It was the first of two extremely fertile stays on the estate – the second followed three years later – known as the 'Boldino autumns', and during the three months of this first period, besides the collection of short stories and two fragments presented here, Pushkin produced the four short plays known as the 'little tragedies' – *The Miserly Knight*, *The Stone Guest*, *Mozart and Salieri* and *A Feast in the Time of Plague*; a comic narrative poem, *The Little House in Kolomna*; some thirty lyric poems; and the concluding chapter of his novel in verse *Eugene Onegin* (as well as working on two other chapters which were eventually excluded from the final text). Add to this a number of critical articles, and it can be appreciated what foresight Pushkin demonstrated when telling his friend Pyotr Pletnyov in a letter written just before he left Moscow for Boldino: 'Autumn is approaching. It's my favourite period – my health usually grows stronger – the time for my literary labours is at hand.'

The Tales of Belkin, to be published anonymously the following year, represent the first work of prose fiction completed by Pushkin, although this was a genre in which he had been testing himself for some time. He had begun a historical novel in the manner of Sir Walter Scott some three years before in 1827, but *The Blackamoor of Peter the Great*, as it was entitled when first published in full after the author's death, a work based on the life of Pushkin's great-grandfather, was abandoned in the middle of the seventh chapter. A novel in letters was begun and left unfinished at the end of 1829, and there exist several other, shorter fragments, almost all produced between *The Blackamoor of Peter the Great* and *The Tales of Belkin*, that show Pushkin's increasing pre-occupation with prose fiction towards the end of the 1820s.

One of the reasons for this concern was certainly the state of the genre in the context of Russian letters as a whole at the time. It was only in the eighteenth century that secular Russian literature developed significantly at all, and it was then dominated by the more elevated genres of the classical hierarchy, all of them in verse. And the so-called Golden Age of Russian literature, the 1820s, was still an age of poetry, albeit very different in nature to that of the previous century, with Pushkin himself and his Pleiad leading the way. The novels and tales that were written in prose over this period were limited in number, and largely limited in quality too, as Russia's most talented writers concentrated on the verse that was so much more prestigious in the tight circles of a national literary world which scarcely extended beyond the gentry class. Pushkin recognised a rare exception in Nikolai Karamzin, whose *Letters of a Russian Traveller* and Sentimental stories of the 1790s allowed Pushkin to answer his own question, 'whose prose is the best in our literature?', with the name of the man whose popularity had enabled him to carry out almost single-handed a reform of the Russian literary language. In his prose, both fictional and later historical, Karamzin used Russian in a way that brought it much closer to French – practically a second native tongue for the Russian upper classes – and thus gave the literary language a flexibility and naturalness that had previously been lacking.

Karamzin was the undisputed leader of the modernising school in Russian literature, and it was inevitable that the innovative Pushkin would follow his example. It was actually in a fragment of a critical article on prose of 1822, one of Pushkin's very earliest such essays, that he declared Karamzin's supremacy, albeit feeling compelled to add, 'yet that is no great praise.' In the same fragment he explained some of his misgivings about Russian prose, and those comments throw a good deal of light on *The Tales of Belkin*. 'But what can be said,' he wrote, 'about our writers who, deeming it low to express the most ordinary things simply, think to enliven their childish prose with additions and limp metaphors? These people will never say *friendship* without adding: that sacred feeling, whose noble flame etc. They ought to say: early in the morning – but they do write: scarcely had the first rays of the rising sun illumined the eastern edges of the azure sky – oh, how new and fresh it all is, except that the only way it's better is that it's longer.' After more amusing examples of unnecessary ornamentation and a word of praise for the style of Voltaire, Pushkin set out his own vision in exemplary fashion: 'Precision and brevity – those are the first virtues of prose. It demands ideas and more ideas – without them, brilliant expressions serve no purpose.'

And it was precisely the style Pushkin recommended here that was put into effect eight years later in *The Tales of Belkin*. The stories have narrative structures of varying degrees of complexity, with, in addition to the numerous internal narrators who make the narratives technically possible, both Ivan Petrovich Belkin himself and the ostensible sources of his narratives (enumerated in the publisher's footnote) intervening between the reader and the events related: but everywhere one can sense the laconic mastery of the actual author. Not a word is wasted, and yet the brevity and simplicity of the narratives belie their subtle intelligence. What seemed to the vast majority of Pushkin's critical contemporaries to be mere bagatelles, presaging the waning of the great poet's powers, were arguably a crucial turning-point in Russian letters, when a verse-dominated literary world was shown ways it could develop the prose fiction that was to make it so influential over the subsequent century and more.

Yet along with his innovative qualities, Pushkin continued to display in *The Tales of Belkin* the protean characteristics which had already been the hallmark of his poetic development. He had shown himself, in, say, *The Fountain of Bakhchisarai* and *Boris Godunov*, capable of learning from writers as different as Byron and Shakespeare, and his distinctive process of adaptation is discernible again in these short stories – to such an extent that they have even been called, in an echo of the contemporaneous 'little tragedies', the 'little parodies'. Both Byron and Shakespeare figure once more, for example as forebears of 'The Shot' and 'Mistress Peasant', but the heroic Byronic outcast is shown in a rather different light in the figure of Silvio, while the Russian Romeo and Juliet enjoy a happier ending than their Italian predecessors. There is a huge literature on *The Tales of Belkin* suggesting numerous different sources of inspiration for the tales, from Washington Irving, through Scott, to Karamzin – the very name of Belkin is suggestive, after all, of busy collection, as *belka* in Russian is a squirrel; but Pushkin's creative reworking of his models made the tales all his own, and proved a vital influence on, say, Lermontov in *A Hero of Our Time* (Silvio, Vulic and

Pechorin) or Dostoevsky in *Poor People* (Devushkin and his reading). It may well be the case that Pushkin's prose, unlike his verse, was overtaken by that of the great Russian writers who followed him, yet its significance should not consequently be undervalued, for Pushkin's legacy as a whole was vital to the shape of the national literature that would emerge onto the world stage after him.

'The History of the Village of Goryukhino' was written at the end of October and the beginning of November 1830 and is generally interpreted in Pushkin scholarship as a pastiche of *The History of the Russian People* (1829–40) by Nikolai Polevoy. Certainly this work was on Pushkin's mind at the time, for he took the newly published second volume with him to Boldino, where he worked on a lengthy but uncompleted review. Polevoy's history was conceived as a response to Karamzin's highly influential *History of the Russian State* (1818–29) – a work which made a considerable impression on Pushkin – and it included much for him to criticise and mock. Indeed, Polevoy's view of national history as being shaped by geography, natural conditions and peoples rather than by outstanding individuals met, perhaps unfairly, with almost universal derision at the time. But as well as being a witty and light-hearted parody of the pretentiously solemn school of historical writing of the age – in his own historical prose Pushkin was subsequently to employ the same stylistic restraint as he did in his fiction – 'The History of the Village of Goryukhino' provided an opportunity to develop further the image of Belkin, its ostensible author. And if in 'his' tales Belkin's voice is diluted by the varying predilections and distinct tones of the four sources from which he is supposed to have gathered them, in his 'History' – and particularly in the introduction, which can be considered complete – we hear him alone for the only time.

The third item in this volume is a fragment dated 26th October 1830, the final remaining piece of fictional prose produced by Pushkin during this first Boldino autumn. Dealing with the life of a poet, it can be considered broadly autobiographical, and it was used in much abbreviated and modified form as part of the characterisation of the poet Charsky in Pushkin's incomplete story 'Egyptian Nights'. Presented here is the image of the writer as a mundane social figure who changes completely when visited by inspiration, an image familiar to readers of Pushkin's verse on the theme of the poet. But the fragment is of interest to the reader of Pushkin's Boldino prose too. Here is a writer inspired and composing prolifically through the autumn months; here is a sketch of a writer whose work is ostensibly to be presented to readers by another; here is a counterweight to Belkin's vision of the man of letters as unattainable demigod. And, most poignant of all from the pen of a poet whose forthcoming marriage would lead to his untimely death in a duel, here is the suggestion that only when fired by inspiration does the writer know true happiness. Pushkin must have been happy indeed at Boldino.

— Hugh Aplin, 2009

The Tales of the Late
Ivan Petrovich Belkin

FROM THE PUBLISHER

MRS PROSTAKOVA: Yes, my dear sir, he's been a lover of stories ever since he was a nipper.
SKOTININ: Mitrofan takes after me.

The Minor[1]

Having undertaken to organise the publication of *The Tales of I.P. Belkin*, which are presented to the public today, we wished to append to the same at least a brief biography of the late author, and thereby to satisfy in part the justifiable curiosity of lovers of our native literature. To this end we thought to turn to Maria Alexeyevna Trafilina, Ivan Petrovich Belkin's closest relative and heiress; but, unfortunately, it was not possible for her to furnish us with any information about him, since she was not in the least acquainted with the deceased. She advised us to address ourselves on this subject to a certain estimable gentleman who had been a friend to Ivan Petrovich. We followed this advice, and received to our letter the following reply, as desired. We include it without any alterations or annotations as a precious memorial to a noble mode of thought and a touching friendship, and, at the same time, as a perfectly adequate biographical notice.

My dear sir, ** **!
I had the honour to receive on the 23rd inst. your most esteemed letter of the 15th inst., wherein you express to me your desire to have a detailed notice of the times of birth and death, the career, the domestic circumstances, and also of the pursuits and disposition of the late Ivan Petrovich Belkin, my former sincere friend and neighbouring landowner. I am fulfilling this, your wish, with great pleasure, and forwarding to you, my dear sir, all that I can call to mind of his conversations, and also of my own observations.

Ivan Petrovich Belkin was born to honest and noble parents in 1798 in the village of Goryukhino. His late father, Second Major Pyotr Ivanovich Belkin, was married to a girl from the house of Trafilin, Pelageya Gavrilovna. He was not a wealthy man, but a moderate one, and in the province of estate management most astute. Their son received his initial education from the village sexton. It was to this estimable man, it seems, that he owed his inclination for reading and pursuits in the province of Russian literature. In 1815 he entered into military service with an infantry regiment of chasseurs (the number I do not recall), in which he remained right up until 1823. The deaths of his parents, which occurred at almost the same time, compelled him to resign his commission and come back to the village of Goryukhino, his patrimony.

Entering into the running of the estate, Ivan Petrovich, by reason of his inexperience and soft-heartedness, in a short time allowed things to fall into neglect and relaxed the strict order established by his late father. Replacing the meticulous and efficient village headman, with whom his peasants (as is their wont) were discontented, he entrusted the running of the village to his old housekeeper, who had gained his trust with her skill in telling stories. This stupid old woman could never distinguish a twenty-five-rouble note from a fifty-rouble one; the peasants, to all of whom she was a gossip, were not in the least afraid of her; the headman they chose pandered to them to such a degree, while behaving at the same time like a rogue, that Ivan Petrovich was obliged to abolish the corvée[2] and introduce a very moderate quit-rent; but even there, exploiting his weakness, the peasants wheedled themselves a significant rebate in the first year, and in the following years paid more than two thirds of the quit-rent in nuts, whortleberries and the like; and there were arrears there too.

Having been a friend to Ivan Petrovich's late father, I considered it my duty to offer my advice to the son as well, and I repeatedly volunteered to restore the former order that he had let slip. To this end, going to visit him once, I demanded the account books, summoned the rogue of a headman, and, in Ivan Petrovich's presence, set about their scrutiny. At first the young master followed me with all possible attention and diligence; but when it became apparent from the accounts that in the previous two years the number of peasants had increased, while the number of farmyard fowl and domesticated livestock had decreased, Ivan Petrovich, satisfied with that first item of information, listened to me no further, and at the very moment when, with my searching and stern interrogation, I had thrown

4

the rogue of a headman into extreme confusion and forced him into utter silence, I heard Ivan Petrovich, to my great annoyance, snoring loudly on his chair. From then on I ceased to intervene in his disposures in husbandry and consigned his affairs (as did he himself) to the disposure of the Almighty.

This did not, however, upset our friendly relations in the least; for, while commiserating with his weakness and pernicious remissness, common to all our young noblemen, I was sincerely fond of Ivan Petrovich; it was, indeed, impossible not to be fond of such a mild and honest young man. For his part, Ivan Petrovich afforded respect to my years and had a heartfelt attachment to me. Right up until his demise he met with me almost every day, holding dear my simple conversation, although we did not for the most part resemble one another in habits, nor in mode of thought, nor in disposition.

Ivan Petrovich led the most moderate life and avoided excess of any kind; I never had occasion to see him tipsy (which in our parts can be considered a wonder unheard-of); for the female sex he had a great inclination, and yet his bashfulness was truly maidenly.[†]

Besides the tales which you are so good as to mention in your letter, Ivan Petrovich left a great number of manuscripts which are in part with me, and have in part been used by his housekeeper for various domestic purposes. Thus, last winter, all the windows in her wing were sealed with the first part of a novel which he had not completed. The aforementioned tales were, it seems, his first endeavour. They are, as Ivan Petrovich used to say, for the most part true, and were heard by him from various persons.[‡] Nonetheless, the names in them were almost all invented by him himself, while the names of the hamlets and villages are borrowed from our neighbourhood, for which reason my village too is somewhere mentioned. This

† There follows an anecdote which we do not include, deeming it superfluous; we assure the reader, however, that it contains nothing detrimental to the memory of Ivan Petrovich Belkin.

‡ In Mr Belkin's manuscript it is indeed written above each tale in the hand of the author: heard by me from *such-and-such a person* (rank or title and initial letters of name and surname). We copy them out for the curiously inquiring: 'The Postmaster' was told to him by Titular Councillor A.G.N., 'The Shot' by Lieutenant-Colonel I.L.P., 'The Undertaker' by the merchant's assistant B.V., 'The Blizzard' and 'Mistress' by Miss K.I.T.

occurred not through some ill intention, but solely through a lack of imagination.

In the autumn of 1828, Ivan Petrovich was taken ill with a cold and temperature, which turned into a high fever, and he died, despite the indefatigable efforts of our district physician, a most skilled man, especially in the treatment of deep-rooted complaints such as corns and the like. He passed away in my arms in his 30th year, and is buried in the church of the village of Goryukhino, close by his late parents.

Ivan Petrovich was of medium height, had grey eyes, light-brown hair, a regular nose; he was white of face and lean.

That, my dear sir, is all I could remember regarding the way of life, pursuits, disposition and appearance of my late neighbour and friend. But in the event of your seeing fit to make any use of this my letter, I beg you most humbly not to mention my name at all; for although I have great respect and fondness for writers, I yet deem entry into that calling superfluous and, at my age, unseemly. With my sincere esteem etc.

26th November 1830
Village of Nenaradovo

Considering it our duty to respect the will of the estimable friend of our author, we tender him our deepest gratitude for the information furnished us, and hope that the public will appreciate its sincerity and kindliness.

A.P.

THE SHOT

> We exchanged shots.
>
> *Baratynsky*[3]

> I swore to shoot him by right of duel
> (he still owed me my shot).
>
> *An Evening on Bivouac*[4]

1

We were stationed in the little town of ***. The life of an army officer is well known. In the morning drill, the riding-school; dinner at the regimental commander's or in a Jewish tavern; in the evening punch and cards. In *** there was not a single open house, not a single eligible girl; we gathered in each other's quarters where, apart from our own tunics, we saw nothing.

Only one man belonged to our society without being in the military. He was about thirty-five, and for that we considered him an old man. Experience gave him many advantages over us; what's more, his habitual gloom, stern temper and sharp tongue had a powerful influence on our young minds. Some sort of mystery surrounded his fate; he seemed to be Russian, but bore a foreign name. He had once served in the hussars, successfully even; nobody knew the reason that had prompted him to resign his commission and settle in a poor little town, where he lived at the same time both poorly and extravagantly: he eternally went about on foot in a threadbare black frockcoat, but kept open house for all the officers of our regiment. True, his dinner consisted of two or three dishes prepared by a retired soldier, but at the same time the champagne flowed in rivers. Nobody knew either his fortune, or his income, and nobody dared ask him about it. He had books, for the most part military ones and novels. He readily lent them out, without ever demanding them back; but then he never returned to its owner any book he had borrowed. His chief exercise consisted in shooting with a pistol. The walls of his room were all eaten away by bullets, covered in holes, like honeycombs. A rich collection of pistols was the only luxury of the poor wattle and daub cottage where he lived. The artistry he had achieved was incredible, and if he had set himself the challenge of knocking a pear off somebody's cap with a bullet, no one in our regiment would have had any doubts about putting his head forward for him. The conversation among us often concerned duels; Silvio (that's what I shall call him) never intervened in it. To the question whether he had ever had occasion to fight a duel, he replied dryly that he had, but he did not go into the details, and it was evident that he found such questions unpleasant. We assumed that there lay upon his conscience some unfortunate victim of his terrible art. In any case, it did not even enter our heads to suspect in him anything like timidity. There are men whose appearance alone dismisses such suspicions. An unexpected occurrence amazed us all.

One day, around ten of our officers were having dinner at Silvio's. We drank in the usual style, that is to say, a very great deal; after dinner we began trying to persuade our host to keep the bank for us at cards. For a long time he refused, as he hardly ever played; finally he ordered the cards to be brought, spilled some fifty gold coins out onto the table and sat down to deal. We surrounded him, and the game got going. Silvio was in the habit of maintaining perfect silence when playing, he never argued and did not explain himself. If a punter happened to miscalculate, he would immediately either pay up the remainder or make a note of the excess. We already knew this and did not prevent him from managing things in his own way; but among us there was an officer who had recently been transferred to us. Playing here too, he had absent-mindedly bent down one corner too many.[5] Silvio took the chalk and made up his account in his habitual way. The officer, thinking he had made a mistake, entered into explanations. Silvio continued to deal. Losing patience, the officer took the brush and wiped out what seemed to him to have been noted down incorrectly. Silvio took the chalk and made a note once again. Inflamed by the wine, the game and the laughter of his comrades, the officer considered himself cruelly offended and, seizing a brass candlestick from the table in a fury, he flung it at Silvio, who barely managed to duck away from the blow. We grew embarrassed. Silvio stood up, pale with anger, and with flashing eyes said, 'Sir, be so good as to leave, and give thanks to God that this happened in my house.'

We did not doubt the consequences and considered our new comrade already a dead man. The officer went away, saying he was ready to answer for the insult however the gentleman banker pleased. The game continued for a few minutes more, but, sensing that our host was in no mood for playing, we fell away, one after the other, and dispersed to our quarters, talking about the imminent vacancy.

The next day in the riding-school we were already asking whether the poor lieutenant was still alive, when he himself appeared among us; we asked him the same question. He replied that he had not yet had any news of Silvio. This amazed us. We went to see Silvio and found him in the yard, putting bullet upon bullet into an ace stuck to the gates. He received us in the usual way, saying not a word about the previous day's occurrence. Three days passed, and the lieutenant was still alive. We asked in amazement: would Silvio really not fight? Silvio did not fight. He contented himself with a very slight explanation and was reconciled.

This might have done him extreme harm in the opinion of the youngsters. A lack of courage is least of all forgiven by young men, who usually see in bravery the summit of human merits and an excuse for all possible vices. However, little by little everything was forgotten, and Silvio gained his former influence once more.

I alone could no longer draw close to him. Having by nature a romantic imagination, I had hitherto been more deeply attached than anyone to a man whose life was a riddle and who seemed to me like the hero of some mysterious tale. He was fond of me; at least, with me alone he would abandon his usual sharp, malicious banter and talk on various subjects with simple-heartedness and unusual pleasantness. But after that unfortunate evening, the thought that his honour had been stained and not washed clean through his own fault, that thought never left me and prevented me from treating him as before; I felt ashamed to look at him. Silvio was too intelligent and experienced not to notice this and not to guess the reason for it. It seemed to grieve him; at least, I noticed in him once or twice a desire to have it out with me; but I avoided such opportunities, and Silvio gave up on me. From that time on, I saw him only in the presence of comrades, and our former frank conversations ceased.

The distracted inhabitants of the capital have no conception of many impressions that are so well known to the inhabitants of villages or small towns, for example, the anticipation of the post day: on Tuesday and Friday our regimental office would be full of officers: some were expecting money, some a letter, some the newspapers. The packets were usually unsealed there and then, news was communicated, and the office presented the most animated picture. Silvio received letters addressed to our regiment, and was usually to be found there too. One day he was handed a packet from which he tore the seal with an air of the greatest impatience. As they ran over the letter, his eyes sparkled. The officers, each occupied with his own letters, noticed nothing. 'Gentlemen,' Silvio said to them, 'circumstances demand my immediate absence; I leave tonight; I hope you won't refuse to dine with me one last time. I expect you too,' he continued, turning to me, 'I expect you without fail.' With these words he hurriedly left; while we, having agreed to meet at Silvio's, dispersed, each in his own direction.

I arrived at Silvio's at the appointed time and found almost the whole regiment there. All of his property was already packed up; only the bare walls with their bullet-holes remained. We sat down at the table; the host was in extremely good spirits, and soon his merriment became universal; corks were continually popping, glasses foamed and fizzed unceasingly, and with all possible zeal we wished the departing man a good journey and every happiness. It was already late in the evening when we rose from the table. As caps were being sorted out, Silvio, saying goodbye to everyone, took me by the arm and stopped me at the very moment when I was preparing to leave. 'I need to have a talk with you,' he said quietly. I remained.

The guests went away; we remained alone, sat down opposite each other and lit our pipes in silence. Silvio was preoccupied; there were no longer any traces of his spasmodic merriment. His gloomy pallor, sparkling eyes and the dense smoke emerging from his mouth lent him the appearance of a genuine devil. Several minutes passed, and Silvio broke the silence.

'We may never see one another again,' he said to me, 'and before parting I wanted to explain myself to you. You may have noticed that I have little respect for the opinions of others; but I'm fond of you, and feel it would be distressing for me to leave an incorrect impression in your mind.'

He paused and started filling his pipe, which had gone out; I was silent, my eyes downcast.

'You found it strange,' he continued, 'that I didn't demand satisfaction from that drunken madcap R***. You must agree that, as I had the choice of weapons, his life was in my hands, while mine was scarcely in danger: I might have ascribed my moderation to magnanimity alone, but I don't want to lie. If I could have punished R*** without exposing my life at all, then not for anything would I have forgiven him.'

I looked at Silvio in amazement. Such an admission had confused me completely. Silvio continued.

'Yes, sir: I don't have the right to expose myself to death. Six years ago I was given a slap in the face, and my enemy is still alive.'

My curiosity was greatly aroused. 'You didn't fight with him?' I asked. 'I suppose circumstances parted you?'

'I did fight with him,' replied Silvio, 'and here's a memento of our duel.'

Silvio stood up and took out of a cardboard box a red hat with a gold tassel and galloon (what the French call a *bonnet de police*[6]); he put it on; there was a bullet-hole in it an inch away from the forehead.

'You know,' Silvio continued, 'that I served in the *** Regiment of Hussars. My character is known to you: I'm used to being number one, but in my youth it was a passion in me. In our days wild behaviour was in fashion: I was the number one firebrand in the army. We boasted of our hard drinking: I outdrank the renowned Burtsov, of whom Denis Davydov sang.[7] Duels took place in our regiment continually; at all of them I was either a witness or an active participant. My comrades adored me, while the regiment's commanding officers, who were continually changing, looked upon me as a necessary evil.

'I was restfully (or restlessly) enjoying my renown, when a young man from a rich and distinguished family (I don't want to name him) joined the regiment. Never in my life have I met a such a brilliantly lucky fellow! Imagine: youth, intelligence, good looks, the most frantic gaiety, the most carefree bravery, a famous name, more money than he could count, money of which he never ran short, and picture for yourself what an effect he must have produced among us. My number one position was shaken. Seduced by my renown, he made to begin seeking my friendship; but I gave him a cold reception, and he distanced himself from me without any regret. I grew to hate him. His successes in the regiment and in the society of women reduced me to utter despair. I started seeking quarrels with him; to my epigrams he replied with ones which always seemed to me more unexpected and wittier than mine and which were, of course, incomparably merrier: he was joking, while I was being malicious. Finally, one day, at a ball in a Polish landowner's house, seeing him to be the object of attention of all the ladies, and especially of the hostess herself, who was involved in a liaison with me, I whispered some coarse vulgarity in his ear. He flared up and gave me a slap in the face. We rushed for our sabres; the ladies all fainted; we were dragged apart, and that same night we went to fight.

'It was at dawn. I was standing at the appointed place with my three seconds. I awaited my adversary with inexpressible impatience. The spring sun had risen, and the heat was already increasing. I caught sight of him at a distance. He was on foot, with his tunic on his sabre, accompanied by one second. We set off towards him. He approached, holding a cap filled with cherries. The seconds measured out twelve paces for us. I ought to have shot first: but the agitation of malice was so great in me that I couldn't rely on the accuracy of my hand and, to give myself time to cool down, I tried to concede the first shot to him; my adversary wouldn't agree. It was proposed to cast lots: the first number fell to him, the eternal favourite of fortune. He took aim and shot through my cap. It was my turn. At last his life was in my hands; I gazed at him greedily, trying to detect at least a shade of disquiet... He stood facing my pistol, picking the ripe cherries out of the cap and spitting out the stones, which flew right as far as me. His indifference infuriated me. What's the use, I thought, of depriving him of his life, when he doesn't hold it at all dear? A malicious thought flashed through my mind. I lowered the pistol. "It seems you can't be bothered with death just now," I said to him, "you wish to have your breakfast; I don't want to disturb you…" – "You're not disturbing me in the least," he objected, "please do shoot, though be it as you wish: you still have your shot; I'm always at your service." I turned to the seconds and announced that I did not intend to shoot that day, and that was how the duel ended.

'I resigned my commission and retired to this little place. Since then, not a single day has passed when I haven't thought about revenge. Now my time has come…'

Silvio took from his pocket the letter he had received in the morning and gave it to me to read. Someone (his attorney, it seemed) had written to him from Moscow that *a certain person* was soon to enter into lawful wedlock with a young and beautiful girl.

'You can guess,' said Silvio, 'who this *certain person* is. I'm going to Moscow. We shall see if he greets death as indifferently just before his wedding as he once awaited it, eating cherries!'

With these words, Silvio rose, threw his cap onto the floor, and began walking backwards and forwards around the room, like a tiger around its cage. I had listened to him motionless; strange, contrasting emotions stirred me.

The servant came in and announced that the horses were ready. Silvio gave my hand a firm squeeze; we kissed. He got into the chaise, where there lay two suitcases, one with his pistols, the other with his belongings. We said goodbye once more, and the horses galloped off.

2

Several years passed, and domestic circumstances compelled me to settle in a poor village in the District of N**. Busy with my husbandry, I did not cease to sigh quietly for my former noisy and carefree life. Most difficult of all for me was getting accustomed to spending the autumn and winter evenings in complete solitude. Until dinner I could still spin out the time one way or another, talking with the village headman, riding out to where work was going on or walking around new farm-buildings; but as soon as it began to get dark, I just did not know what to do with myself. I knew by heart the small number of books I had found underneath cupboards and in the storeroom. All the folk tales that the housekeeper Kirilovna could possibly remember had been retold me; the peasant women's songs made me feel depressed. I was on the verge of taking to unsweetened fruit liqueur, only it gave me a headache; and I confess, I was afraid of becoming a *drunkard from sorrow*, i.e. the very *sorriest* of drunkards, of whom I had seen a host of examples in our District. There were no close neighbours anywhere near me, except for two or three *sorry* ones, whose conversation consisted for the most part of hiccoughs and sighs. Solitude was more tolerable.[8]

Four kilometres from me there was a rich estate belonging to Countess B***; but only the steward lived there, and the Countess had visited her estate only once, in the first year of her marriage, and even then had stayed there for no more than a month. However, in the second spring of my seclusion the rumour spread that the Countess and her husband would be coming to their village for the summer. And they did indeed arrive at the beginning of June.

The arrival of a rich neighbour is an important epoch for country-dwellers. Landowners and their house-serfs talk about it for a couple of months beforehand, and for about three years afterwards. As far as I am concerned, I confess that the news of the arrival of a young and beautiful neighbour had a powerful effect upon me; I burned with impatience to see her, and so, on the first Sunday after her arrival, I set off after lunch for the village of *** to introduce myself to their Highnesses as their nearest neighbour and most humble servant.

A footman led me into the Count's study, and went off himself to announce me. The spacious study was decorated with all possible luxury; by the walls stood bookcases, and above each one was a bronze bust; above the marble fireplace was a wide mirror; the floor was upholstered in green cloth and covered with rugs. Being unaccustomed to luxury in my poor corner, and not having seen anyone else's wealth in a long time by then, I grew timid and awaited the Count with a certain trepidation, as a petitioner from the provinces awaits the emergence of a minister. The doors opened, and in came a very good-looking man of about thirty-two. The Count approached me with an open and friendly air; I tried to take heart and was about to begin introducing myself, but he forestalled me. We sat down. His conversation, free and courteous, soon dispelled the shyness I had developed in the wilds; I was already starting to get back into my usual condition, when suddenly in came the Countess, and confusion took hold of me worse than before. She was indeed a beauty. The Count introduced me; I wanted to seem free and easy, but the more I tried to take upon myself an air of unconstraint, the more awkward I felt. To give me time to recover and grow accustomed to the new acquaintanceship, they began talking between themselves, treating me like a good neighbour, without ceremony. I, meanwhile, began walking backwards and forwards, examining the books and the pictures. I am no connoisseur of pictures, but one did attract my attention. It depicted some scene from Switzerland, yet it was not the way it was painted that struck me about it, but the fact that the picture had had two bullets shot through it, one planted on top of the other.

'That was a good shot,' I said, addressing the Count.

'Yes,' he replied, 'a very remarkable shot. And do you shoot well?' he continued.

'Tolerably well,' I replied, glad that the conversation had finally touched upon a subject dear to me. 'I wouldn't miss a card at thirty paces, not with pistols I'm familiar with, of course.'

'Really?' said the Countess with an air of great attentiveness. 'And you, my dear, would you hit a card at thirty paces?'

'Some day,' replied the Count, 'we'll give it a try. I wasn't a bad shot in my time, but it's four years now since I last picked up a pistol.'

'Oh,' I remarked, 'in that case I wager your Highness wouldn't hit a card even at twenty paces: the pistol demands daily practice. That I know from experience. I was considered one of the best shots in our regiment. I once had occasion not to pick up a pistol for a whole month: mine were being repaired; and what do you think, your Highness? The first time I started shooting afterwards, I missed a bottle at twenty-five paces four times running. We had a captain, a wit, a humorist; he happened to be there, and he said to me: you evidently can't bear to do harm to a bottle, old chap. No, your Highness, you shouldn't neglect that practice, otherwise get out of the habit is what you will. The best shot I was lucky enough to meet used to shoot every day, at least three times before dinner. It was a habit with him, like a glass of vodka.'

The Count and Countess were pleased I had warmed to my theme.

'And what was his shooting like?' the Count asked me.

'It was like this, your Highness: it sometimes happened that he'd see a fly settle on a wall: you're laughing, Countess? Honest to God, it's true. It sometimes happened that he'd see a fly and shout: "Kuzka, my pistol!" And so Kuzka brings him a loaded pistol. Bang, and he'd squash the fly against the wall!'

'That's amazing!' said the Count. 'And what was his name?'

'Silvio, your Highness.'

'Silvio!' exclaimed the Count, leaping up from his seat. 'You knew Silvio?'

'Of course I did, your Highness; he and I were friends; he was received in our regiment as one of us, a comrade; but it's already five years or so now since I last had any news of him. So your Highness used to know him too then?'

'I did, I knew him very well. Did he not tell you the story… but no, I doubt it; did he not tell you the story of one very strange occurrence?'

'You don't mean the slap in the face, your Highness, that he got at a ball from some young rake?'

'And did he ever tell you the name of that young rake?'

'No, your Highness, he never did… Oh! Your Highness,' I continued, guessing the truth, 'forgive me… I didn't know… was it you then?…'

'I myself,' replied the Count with an extremely disconcerted air, 'and the picture with the bullet holes in it is a memento of our last meeting…'

'Oh darling,' said the Countess, 'for God's sake don't tell the story; I'll be terrified listening to it.'

'No,' retorted the Count, 'I'll tell the whole story; he knows how I insulted his friend, so let him learn how Silvio had his revenge on me.'

The Count drew up an armchair for me, and with the liveliest curiosity I heard the following story.

'Five years ago I got married. The first month, *the honeymoon*, I spent here in this village. I'm indebted to this house for the best moments of my life and for one of the most difficult memories.

'One evening we were out riding together; my wife's horse turned obstinate for some reason; she took fright, handed the reins over to me and set off for home on foot; I rode on ahead. In the yard I saw a travelling carriage; I was told there was a man sitting in my study who hadn't wanted to give his name, but who had simply said that he had some business with me. I came into this room, and in the darkness saw a man covered in dust and with a growth of beard; he was standing here by the fireplace. I approached him, trying to place his features. "Don't you recognise me, Count?" he said in a quavering voice. "Silvio!" I cried, and, I confess, I felt my hair suddenly standing on end. "Yes, sir," he continued, "it's my shot; I've come to discharge my pistol; are you ready?" He had a pistol poking out of his side pocket. I measured out twelve paces and stood over there in the corner, asking him to shoot quickly, before my wife came back. He took his time – he asked for some light. Candles were brought. I closed the doors, ordered that no one enter and again asked him to shoot. He pulled out the pistol and took aim… I was counting the seconds… I was thinking of her… A terrible minute passed! Silvio lowered his hand. "'I'm sorry," he said, "that the pistol isn't loaded with cherry stones… the bullet's heavy. I keep on thinking that what we have here isn't a duel, but murder: I'm not used to aiming at an unarmed man. We'll start afresh; we'll cast lots for who's to shoot first." My head was spinning… I don't think I agreed… Finally we loaded another pistol; rolled up two lots; he put them into the cap I had once shot a hole through; again I took out the first number. "You, Count, have the luck of the Devil," he said, with a grin I shall never forget. I don't understand what was wrong with me, and how he could have forced me into it… but – I shot, and hit this picture here.' (The Count pointed to the picture with the bullet-holes in it; his face was burning like fire; the Countess was paler than her handkerchief: I was unable to refrain from an exclamation.)

'I shot,' the Count continued, 'and, thank God, I missed; then Silvio… (he was at that moment truly terrible) Silvio started to take aim at me. Suddenly the doors opened, Masha runs in and, with a shriek, throws herself on my neck. Her presence restored all my courage to me. "Darling," I said to her, "can't you see that we're having a joke? What a fright you've had! Go and drink a glass of water and come back to us; I'll introduce an old friend and comrade to you." Masha still couldn't believe it. "Tell me, is what my husband's saying true?" she said, addressing the threatening Silvio, "is it true that you're both having a joke?" – "He's always having a joke, Countess," Silvio answered her; "once he gave me a slap in the face for a joke, for a joke he shot a hole through this cap here for me, for a joke he missed hitting me just now; now I feel the urge to have a joke too…" With these words he went to take aim at me… in front of her! Masha threw herself at his feet. "Get up, Masha, for shame!" I cried in fury, "and you, sir, will you stop making fun of a poor woman? Will you shoot or not?" – "I won't," replied Silvio, "I'm content: I've seen your confusion, your timidity, I've made you shoot at me, I've done enough. You'll remember me. I leave you to your conscience." At that point he made to leave, but stopped in the doorway, glanced back at the picture I had shot the bullet through, fired at it, almost without taking aim, and disappeared. My wife lay in a faint; the servants didn't dare stop him and gazed at him in horror; he went out onto the porch, called to the coachman and drove off before I'd had time to come to my senses.'

The Count fell silent. Thus I learnt the end of the tale, whose beginning had once so astonished me. With its hero I met no more. They say that during Alexander Ypsilantis' rebellion, Silvio led a detachment of Eteria men and was killed at the Battle of Skouliani.[9]

Steeds are racing over mounds
Trampling snow deep-lying…
Over there's a house of God,
Solitary standing.
. . . . .
Suddenly the blizzard blows;
Snow comes down in blankets;
Wings outspread, a raven black
Spirals o'er the sleigh now;
Sorrow's what its cry foretells!
Steeds in haste and nervous
Peer into the distance dark,
Manes on end and bristling…

Zhukovsky[10]

At the end of 1811, in an era memorable for us Russians,[11] good Gavrila Gavrilovich R** was living on his estate of Nenaradovo. He was famed throughout the district for his hospitality and cordiality; his neighbours were continually visiting him for something to eat, to drink, to play Boston for five kopeks a time with his wife, and some in order to gaze at their daughter, Maria Gavrilovna, a slim, pale, seventeen-year-old girl. She was considered a wealthy potential bride, and many intended her for themselves or for their sons.

Maria Gavrilovna had been raised on French novels, and con-sequently was in love. The object she had chosen was a poor army ensign who was on leave in his village. It goes without saying that the young man burned with an equal passion, and that the parents of his beloved, remarking their mutual inclination, forbade their daughter even to think of him, and gave him a worse reception than the retired magistrate.

Our lovers were in correspondence, and every day they met alone in the pine grove or by the old chapel. There they swore eternal love to one another, lamented their fate and made all sorts of plans. Corresponding and conversing in this way, they reached (as is quite natural) the following argument: if we cannot breathe without one another, but the will of cruel parents stands in the way of our happiness, then can we not do without them? It stands to reason that this happy thought occurred to the young man first and that it was much to the liking of Maria Gavrilovna's romantic imagination.

Winter arrived and put an end to their rendezvous, but the correspondence became all the more lively. Vladimir Nikolayevich implored her in every letter to put herself into his hands, for them to marry in secret, disappear for a certain time, then throw themselves down at the feet of her parents, who would, of course, at last be touched by the heroic constancy and misfortune of the lovers and would be sure to say to them: 'Children! Come to our arms!'

Maria Gavrilovna wavered for a long time; a multitude of plans for flight were rejected. Finally she consented: on the appointed day she was not to eat supper, but to retire to her room on the pretext of a headache. Her maid was in the conspiracy; both of them were to go out into the garden through the back porch, to find beyond the garden the sleigh that had been prepared, to get into it and ride five kilometres from Nenaradovo to the village of Zhadrino, straight to the church, where Vladimir was already to be waiting for them.

On the eve of the decisive day, Maria Gavrilovna was awake all night; she was packing, tying up bundles of linen and clothing, and she wrote a long letter to a young lady of sentiment, her friend, and another to her parents. She bade them farewell in the most touching terms, excused her misdemeanour by the insuperable power of passion, and ended that she would deem it the most blissful moment of her life when she was permitted to throw herself at the feet of her dearest parents. Having sealed both letters with a signet made in Tula, on which were depicted two burning hearts with a seemly inscription, she threw herself onto her bed just before dawn and dozed off; but even then terrible dreams constantly woke her up. First it would seem to her that at the very moment when she was getting into the sleigh to go and get married, her father stopped her, dragged her with agonising speed across the snow and threw her into a dark, bottomless cellar... and she flew headlong with an inexpressible sinking of the heart; then she would see Vladimir, lying on some grass, pale and bloodied. Dying, he begged her in a piercing voice to hurry up and marry him... other shocking, senseless visions drifted before her one after another. Finally she got up, paler than usual and with an unfeigned headache. Her father and mother noticed her disquiet; their tender solicitude and unceasing questions: what's the matter, Masha? are you ill, Masha? rent her heart. She tried to reassure them, to seem cheerful, and could not. Evening came on. The idea that she was spending the day in the midst of her family for the last time now constricted her heart. She was barely alive; she was secretly saying goodbye to all the people, to all the objects that surrounded her.

Supper was served; her heart began beating hard. In a tremulous voice she announced that she did not feel like having supper, and began taking her leave of her father and mother. They kissed and, as usual, blessed her: she almost burst out crying. Entering her room, she flung herself into an armchair and dissolved in tears. The maid tried to persuade her to calm down and take courage. Everything was ready. In half an hour Masha was to leave her parental home, her room, her quiet, maidenly life for ever... Outside there was a blizzard; the wind howled, the shutters shook and rattled; everything seemed to her a threat and a sorrowful augury. All in the house soon grew quiet and fell asleep. Masha wrapped herself up in a shawl, put on a warm housecoat, picked up her casket and went out onto the back porch. The maidservant followed her, carrying two bundles. They went down into the garden. The blizzard was not abating; the wind was blowing against them, as though in an effort to stop the young transgressor. It was an effort for them to reach the end of the garden. The sleigh was waiting for them on the road. The horses, frozen through, would not stand still; Vladimir's coachman was pacing about in front of the shafts, restraining the eager creatures. He helped the young lady and her maid to take their seats and stow away the bundles and the casket, he took up the reins, and the horses flew off. Entrusting the young lady to the care of fate and the skill of Tereshka the coachman, we shall turn to our other young lover.

Vladimir had been on his travels the whole day. In the morning he had been with the Zhadrino priest; it had been a struggle to reach an agreement with him; then he had gone to look for witnesses from among the neighbouring landowners. The first he came to, the forty-year-old retired cornet Dravin, agreed willingly. This adventure, he avowed, reminded him of former times and hussars' pranks. He had persuaded Vladimir to stay and have dinner with him, and assured him that finding the other two witnesses would not present any problem. Indeed, immediately after dinner there had appeared the land-surveyor Schmidt, wearing whiskers and spurs, and the son of the police captain, a boy of about sixteen who had recently joined the uhlans. Not only had they accepted Vladimir's proposition, they had even sworn their readiness to sacrifice their lives for him. Vladimir had embraced them in delight and gone home to get ready.

It had already long been growing dark. He sent his reliable Tereshka off to Nenaradovo with his troika and with detailed, circumstantial instructions, and he ordered the little one-horse sledge to be harnessed for himself, and set off alone, without a coachman, for Zhadrino, where Maria Gavrilovna was also due to arrive in about two hours' time. The road was familiar to him, and it was only a twenty-minute ride.

But scarcely had Vladimir driven out of the village into the open than the wind rose and such a blizzard blew up that he could not see a thing. The road was under snow in a minute; the surroundings disappeared in a murky and yellowish haze, through which flew white flakes of snow; the sky merged with the earth. Vladimir found himself in the fields and tried in vain to get back onto the road; the horse stepped out haphazardly and was continually either mounting a snow-drift or falling into a pit; the sledge was continually tipping over. Vladimir strove simply not to lose the right direction. But it seemed to him that more than half an hour had already passed, and still he had not reached the Zhadrino grove. About another ten minutes passed; still the grove was nowhere to be seen. Vladimir was driving across a field crisscrossed by deep gullies. The blizzard was not dying down, the sky was not clearing. The horse was beginning to tire, while he himself was sweating profusely, despite the fact that he was continually waist-deep in snow.

Finally he saw that he was driving the wrong way. Vladimir stopped: he started to think, remember, consider – and persuaded himself that he should have borne to the right. He set off to the right. His horse could hardly walk. He had already been travelling for more than an hour. Zhadrino ought to have been not far off. But he drove and drove, and there was no end to the fields. Just snow-drifts and gullies; the sledge was continually tipping over, he was continually picking it up. Time was passing; Vladimir was beginning to get very worried.

Finally, to one side, something showed up black. Vladimir turned that way. Coming closer, he saw the grove. Thank God, he thought, it's not far now. He went up close to the grove, hoping to get onto the familiar road at once or to skirt around the grove: Zhadrino was immediately beyond it. Soon he found the road and drove into the gloom of the trees, denuded by the winter. The wind could not rage here; the road was smooth; the horse took courage and Vladimir calmed down.

But he drove and drove, and Zhadrino was nowhere to be seen; there was no end to the grove. Vladimir saw in horror that he had driven into an unfamiliar wood. Despair took hold of him. He struck the horse; the poor animal made to go at a trot, but soon began to tire, and in a quarter of an hour was at a walk, despite all the efforts of the unhappy Vladimir.

Little by little the trees began to thin, and Vladimir drove out of the wood; Zhadrino was nowhere to be seen. It must have been around midnight. Tears splashed from his eyes; he set off at random. The weather had quietened down, the storm-clouds were dispersing, and before him lay a plain, covered with a white, undulating carpet. The night was quite clear. Not far off he caught sight of a little village consisting of four or five homesteads. Vladimir drove towards it. At the first little hut he jumped out of the sledge, ran up to the window and started knocking. After a few minutes, the wooden shutter lifted, and an old man poked his grey beard out. 'Whadya want?' – 'Is it far to Zhadrino?' – 'Is it far to *Zhadrino*?' – 'Yes, yes! Is it far?' – 'No, not far; it'll be ten kilometres or so.' At this reply, Vladimir grabbed himself by the hair and remained motionless, like a man condemned to death.

'And where are yer from?' the old man continued. Vladimir did not have the heart to answer questions. 'Old man,' he said, 'can you get me horses to go to Zhadrino?' – 'What 'orses are we gonna 'ave?' replied the peasant. 'Well, can I at least take a guide? I'll pay, however much he wants.' – "Ang on,' said the old man, lowering the blind, 'I'll send me son out to yer; 'e'll guide yer.' Vladimir began waiting. Not a minute had passed before he started knocking again. The shutter was lifted, the beard appeared. 'Whadya want?' – 'What about your son?' – ''E'll be out in a minute, 'e's puttin' on 'is boots. Frozen, are yer? Come in and get warm.' – 'Thank you, just send your son out quickly.'

The gates creaked; a lad with a cudgel came out and set off in front, now indicating, now searching for the road, which was covered with snow-drifts. 'What's the time?' Vladimir asked him. 'It'll soon be dawn,' the young peasant replied. Vladimir did not say another word.

The cocks were crowing and it was already light when they reached Zhadrino. The church was locked. Vladimir paid his guide and drove to the priest's yard. His troika was not in the yard. What news awaited him!

But let us return to the good Nenaradovo landowners and see what is going on there.

Not a thing.

The old couple woke up and emerged into the drawing room. Gavrila Gavrilovich is wearing a cap and a flannelette jacket. Praskovya Petrovna is wearing a wadded housecoat. The samovar was brought, and Gavrila Gavrilovich sent the girl to find out from Maria Gavrilovna how her health was and how she had slept. The girl came back announcing that the young mistress said she'd slept badly, but that she was feeling better now, and she'd be coming to the drawing room right away. Indeed, the door opened, and Maria Gavrilovna came up to greet her Papa and Mama.

'How's your head, Masha?' asked Gavrila Gavrilovich. 'Better, Papa,' replied Masha. 'It must have been the fumes from the stove yesterday, Masha,' said Praskovya Petrovna. 'Perhaps, Mama,' replied Masha.

The day went by well enough, but in the night Masha was taken ill. They sent into town for the doctor. He came towards evening and found the sick girl delirious. A high fever developed, and for two weeks the poor sick girl was at death's door.

Nobody in the house knew of the proposed flight. The letters she had written on the day before had been burnt; her chambermaid did not tell anyone anything, fearing the anger of the master and mistress. The priest, the retired cornet, the bewhiskered land-surveyor and the little uhlan were reticent, and not without reason. Tereshka the coachman never let anything superfluous out, even when tight. Thus the secret was kept by more than half a dozen conspirators. But Maria Gavrilovna, incessantly delirious, let her secret out herself. However, her words were so utterly incongruous that her mother, who did not leave her bedside, was able to understand from them only the fact that her daughter was fatally enamoured of Vladimir Nikolayevich, and that love was probably the cause of her illness. She took counsel with her husband and with several neighbours, and everyone at last unanimously decided that this was evidently Maria Gavrilovna's fate, that you can't ride around your intended on a horse, that poverty isn't a crime, that it's not wealth you have to live with but a man, and so on. Moral adages can be amazingly useful in instances when we ourselves can come up with but little in our justification.

In the meantime, the young mistress began to recover. Vladimir had not been seen for a long time in Gavrila Gavrilovich's house. He had been scared off by the way he was usually received. It was proposed to send for him and advise him of his unexpected good fortune: consent to marriage. But what was the astonishment of the Nenaradovo landowners when, in response to their invitation, they received from him a half-crazy letter! He declared to them that he would never set foot in their house, and asked them to forget the unfortunate for whom the last remaining hope was death. A few days later they learnt that Vladimir had left for the army. This was in 1812.

For a long time they did not dare tell the convalescent Masha of this. She never mentioned Vladimir. Several months later, on finding his name in the list of those who had been severely wounded while distinguishing themselves at Borodino,[12] she fainted, and it was feared her fever might return. Her fainting fit, however, had no consequences, thank God.

She was visited by another sadness: Gavrila Gavrilovich passed away, leaving her as the heiress to his entire estate. But the inheritance did not console her; she shared sincerely in the grief of poor Praskovya Petrovna, and swore never to be parted from her; they both left Nenaradovo, a place of sad memories, and went to live on their estate in ***.

Here too, suitors circled around the pretty, wealthy, marriageable girl, but she gave no one so much as the slightest hope. Her mother sometimes tried to persuade her to choose herself a husband; Maria Gavrilovna would shake her head and become pensive. Vladimir no longer existed: he had died in Moscow on the eve of the entry of the French. His memory seemed sacred for Masha; at least, she kept safe everything that might remind her of him: the books he had once read, his drawings, the music and poetry he had copied out for her. The neighbours, when they learnt about everything, wondered at her constancy and awaited with curiosity the hero who was intended to triumph at last over the sad fidelity of this virginal Artemisia.[13]

In the meantime the war had come to a glorious end. Our regiments were returning from abroad. The people rushed to meet them. Bands played songs taken in war: *Vive Henri-Quatre*,[14] Tyrolean waltzes and arias from *Joconde*.[15] Officers who had gone off on campaign as little more than adolescents were returning as men, matured in the martial air and festooned with medals. Soldiers conversed cheerfully amongst themselves, constantly mixing German and French words in with their speech. An unforgettable time! A time of glory and rapture! How hard did a Russian heart beat at the word *Fatherland*! How sweet were the tears of reunion! With what unanimity did we combine feelings of national pride and love for the Sovereign! And what a moment it was for him![16]

Women, Russian women, were incomparable then. Their usual coldness vanished. Their rapture was truly intoxicating when, greeting the conquerors, they cried: *hurrah!*

And threw their bonnets in the air.[17]

Who of the officers of that time does not acknowledge that he was indebted to a Russian woman for his best, most precious reward?…

At this brilliant time, Maria Gavrilovna was living with her mother in the Province of *** and did not see the way the two capitals celebrated the return of the troops. But in provincial towns and villages the general rapture was, perhaps, even greater. It was a genuine triumph for an officer when he appeared in such places, and a lover in a frockcoat came off badly in his vicinity.

We have already said that, in spite of her coldness, Maria Gavrilovna was still surrounded, as before, by seekers. But all had to retreat when there appeared in her castle the wounded colonel of hussars Burmin, with the George Cross in his buttonhole and *with an interesting pallor*, as the young ladies of those parts used to say. He was about twenty-six years old. He had come on leave to his estates, which were in the neighbourhood of Maria Gavrilovna's village. Maria Gavrilovna very much singled him out. In his presence her usual pensiveness would be enlivened. It could not be said that she flirted with him; but a poet, noticing her behaviour, would have said:

Se amor non è, che dunque?...[18]

Burmin was, indeed, a very nice young man. He had precisely the mind that women like: a mind decorous and observant, without any pretensions, and casually mocking. His behaviour with Maria Gavrilovna was straightforward and relaxed; but whatever she said or did, his soul and gaze just followed her. He seemed to be of a quiet and modest disposition, but rumour had it that he had once been a terrible rake, and this did him no harm in the opinion of Maria Gavrilovna, who (like all young ladies generally) gladly excused any mischief that revealed a bold and ardent character.

But more than anything... (more than his gentleness, more than his pleasant conversation, more than his interesting pallor, more than his bandaged arm) it was the silence of the young hussar that excited her curiosity and imagination more than anything. She could not help but be aware that he liked her very much; he too, with his intelligence and experience, could probably already have noticed that she favoured him: so how was it she had not yet seen him at her feet and not yet heard his confession of love? What was holding him back? The timidity that is inseparable from true love, pride, or the coquetry of a cunning philanderer? This was a riddle for her. After having a good think, she decided that timidity was the only reason for it, and resolved to encourage him with greater attentiveness and, depending on circumstances, even tenderness. She was preparing a most unexpected denouement, and awaited with impatience the moment of romantic declaration. A secret, of whatever sort it might be, is always burdensome for the female heart. Her military action had the desired success:

at least, Burmin fell into such pensiveness, and his black eyes would fix on Maria Gavrilovna with such fire that the decisive moment, it seemed, was already near. The neighbours spoke of the wedding as of a matter already settled, and good Praskovya Petrovna rejoiced that her daughter had finally found herself a worthy suitor.

One day, the old woman was sitting alone in the drawing room playing grand patience, when Burmin entered the room and immediately enquired about Maria Gavrilovna. 'She's in the garden,' the old woman replied, 'go to her, and I'll wait here for you.' Burmin went, and the old woman crossed herself, thinking: perhaps the matter will be settled today!

Burmin found Maria Gavrilovna by the pond, under a weeping willow, with a book in her hands and in a white dress, like a true heroine from a novel. After the first questions, Maria Gavrilovna deliberately gave up sustaining the conversation, thus intensifying the mutual embarrassment which could perhaps only be resolved by a sudden and decisive declaration. And that is what took place: sensing the difficulty of his position, Burmin announced that he had long been seeking an opportunity to open up his heart to her, and demanded a moment's attention. Maria Gavrilovna closed the book and lowered her eyes to signify consent.

'I love you,' said Burmin, 'I love you passionately...' (Maria Gavrilovna blushed, and bent her head still lower.) 'I have acted incautiously, surrendering myself to sweet habit, the habit of daily seeing and hearing you...' (Maria Gavrilovna recalled Saint-Preux's first letter.[19]) 'It's too late now to resist my fate; the memory of you, your dear, incomparable image will henceforth be the agony and the delight of my life; but it still remains for me to fulfil an onerous obligation, to disclose to you a terrible secret and to put an insuperable obstacle between us...' – 'It has always existed,' Maria Gavrilovna interrupted with animation, 'I could never have been your wife...' – 'I know,' he answered her quietly, 'I know that once you loved, but death and three years of lamentations... Good, dear Maria Gavrilovna! Don't try to deprive me of my last consolation: the thought that you would have consented to bring about my happiness, if... say nothing, for God's sake, say nothing. You're torturing me. Yes, I know, I sense that you would have been mine, but – I'm the unhappiest of creatures… I'm married!'

Maria Gavrilovna glanced up at him in surprise.

'I'm married,' Burmin continued, 'I've been married for more than three years, and I don't know who my wife is, or where she is, or whether I might some day have to meet with her!'

'What are you saying?' exclaimed Maria Gavrilovna, 'how strange it is! Carry on; I'll tell my story afterwards… but be so kind as to carry on.'

'At the beginning of 1812,' said Burmin, 'I was hurrying to Vilna where our regiment was. Arriving at a posting station late one evening, I was on the point of ordering horses to be harnessed quickly, when suddenly a terrible blizzard got up, and the postmaster and the drivers advised me to wait it out. I heeded their advice, but an incomprehensible disquiet took hold of me; someone seemed to be simply pushing me on. In the meantime, the blizzard was not abating; I lost patience, ordered the horses to be harnessed again, and set off into the midst of the storm. The driver took it into his head to go along the river, which ought to have shortened our journey by three kilometres. The banks were covered in snow; the driver went past the spot where you came out onto the road, and thus we found ourselves in unfamiliar parts. The storm was not dying down; I caught sight of a little light and ordered the driver to go that way. We arrived in a village; there was light in the wooden church. The church was open, and behind the fence stood several sleighs; people were walking about in the porch. "Over here! Over here!" cried several voices. I ordered the driver to drive over. "I say, where did you get delayed?" someone said to me. "The bride's fainted; the priest doesn't know what to do; we were ready to go back. Hurry up and get out." I jumped out of the sleigh in silence and entered the church, dimly lit by two or three candles. A young girl was sitting on a bench in a dark corner of the church; another was rubbing her temples. "Thank God," this one said, "you've just about made it. You've all but been the death of the young mistress." The old priest came up to me with a question: "Do you want us to begin?" – "Yes, do begin, Father," I replied absentmindedly. The girl was helped up. She seemed to me not bad-looking… Incomprehensible, unforgivable frivolousness… I stood next to her before the lectern; the priest was in a hurry; the three men and the maidservant were supporting the bride and were concerned only with her. We were married. "Kiss one another," we were told. My wife turned her pale face towards me. I was about to kiss her… She cried out: "Oh, it's not him! It's not him!" and fell down unconscious. The witnesses fastened frightened eyes upon me. I turned, walked out of the church without any hindrance, threw myself into the *kibitka* and cried: "Drive on!"'

'My God!' cried Maria Gavrilovna. 'And you don't know what became of your poor wife?'

'I don't,' Burmin replied, 'I don't know the name of the village where I was married; I don't remember which posting station I went from. At the time I attached so little importance to my criminal prank that, after driving off from the church, I fell asleep and woke up the next morning when already at the third posting station. The servant who was with me then died on campaign, and so I don't have even a hope of finding the woman I made sport of so cruelly, and who is now so cruelly avenged.'

'My God, my God!' said Maria Gavrilovna, seizing his hand, 'so it was you! And don't you recognise me?'

Burmin turned pale… and threw himself down at her feet…

THE UNDERTAKER

Do we not daily coffins see,
The universe decrepit's greying?

Derzhavin[20]

The last of the undertaker Adrian Prokhorov's belongings were loaded
up onto the hearse, and for the fourth time the skinny pair of horses
dragged itself from Basmannaya to Nikitskaya, which was where the
undertaker and his entire household were moving. Locking up the
shop, he nailed an advertisement to the gates about the house being for
sale and to let, and he set off on foot for his new home. Approaching
the little yellow house, which had been seducing his imagination for
such a long time and which he had finally bought for a considerable
sum, the old undertaker was surprised to feel that his heart was not
rejoicing. Stepping across the unfamiliar threshold and finding bedlam
in his new dwelling, he sighed for the little tumbledown shack where,
over the course of eighteen years, everything had been arranged in the
strictest order; he started scolding both of his daughters and the
domestic for their slowness, and set about helping them himself. Order
was soon established; the icon-case with the icons, the cabinet with
the crockery, the table, the couch and the bed occupied the corners
assigned to them in the rear room; in the kitchen and the sitting room
were the master's wares: coffins of all colours and every size, and also
cupboards with funeral hats, cloaks and torches. Above the gates rose
a signboard depicting a plump Cupid with a torch held upside down
and with the inscription: 'Plain and painted coffins sold and upholstered here, also rented out and old ones repaired.' The girls went off
to their front room. Adrian made a tour of his dwelling, sat down by the
window and ordered the samovar to be prepared.

The enlightened reader is aware that Shakespeare and Walter Scott
both represented their gravediggers[21] as cheerful and humorous people
so as to strike our imaginations the more powerfully with this contrast. Out of respect for the truth, we cannot follow their example and
are forced to admit that our undertaker's disposition corresponded
perfectly to his sombre trade. Adrian Prokhorov was generally gloomy

and pensive. He would break his silence perhaps only to take his daughters to task when he caught them staring idly out of the window at passers-by, or to ask an exaggerated price for his works of those who had the misfortune (or sometimes even the pleasure) of needing them. And so Adrian, sitting at the window and drinking his seventh cup of tea, was, as usual, sunk in sad reflections. He thought about the torrential rain which, a week before, had greeted the funeral of a retired brigadier at the very gates of the city. Many of the cloaks had shrunk because of it, many of the hats had gone crooked. He foresaw un-avoidable outlay, for his long-held stock of funeral attire was getting into a pitiful state. He hoped to compensate for the losses with old Tryukhina, the merchant's wife, who had already been on the point of death for about a year. But Tryukhina was dying on Razgulyai, and Prokhorov was afraid that her heirs, despite their promise, might be too lazy to send for him at such a distance and might agree terms with the nearest contractor.

These reflections were unexpectedly cut short by three Masonic knocks on the door. 'Who's that?' asked the undertaker. The door opened, and into the room came a man in whom at first glance could be recognised a German tradesman, and he approached the undertaker with a cheerful air. 'Excuse me, dear neighbour,' he said in that Russian dialect which to this day we are unable to hear without laughter, 'excuse me for disturbing you... I wanted straight away to make your acquaintance. I am a cobbler, my name is Gottlieb Scchultz, and I live across the street from you, in the little house that is opposite your windows. I am celebrating tomorrow my silver wedding, and I beg you and your daughters to have with me dinner as friends.' The invitation was graciously accepted. The undertaker asked the cobbler to sit down and have a cup of tea, and, thanks to Gottlieb Schultz's open dis-position, they soon got into amicable conversation. 'How's business for your good self?' asked Adrian. 'O-ho-ho,' replied Schultz, 'it comes and it goes. I cannot complain. Although, of course, my goods are not like yours: a living man can manage without boots, but a dead man cannot live without a coffin.' – 'Quite true,' remarked Adrian, 'however, if a living man hasn't the wherewithal to buy boots, then, begging your pardon, he goes around barefooted; but a dead beggar gets himself a coffin for free.' Their conversation continued in this vein for some time yet; finally the cobbler got up and took his leave of the undertaker, renewing his invitation.

Next day, at exactly twelve o'clock, the undertaker and his daughters went out of the gate of their newly bought house and set off for their neighbour's. I shall not begin to describe either Adrian Prokhorov's Russian caftan, or the European costumes of Akulina and Darya, departing in this instance from the custom adopted by present-day novelists. I do not, however, think it superfluous to remark that both girls put on yellow hats and red shoes, something they did only on ceremonial occasions.

The cobbler's cramped little quarters were filled with guests, German tradesmen for the most part, with their wives and apprentices. The only Russian official there was the constable, Jurko, a Finn, who had managed, despite his humble rank, to win the particular favour of the host. For some twenty-five years he had done service faithful and true in this rank, like Pogorelsky's postman.[22] The fire of 1812, which devastated Russia's first capital, destroyed his yellow sentry-box too. But immediately upon the expulsion of the enemy, there appeared in its place a new one, grey, with little white Doric columns, and Jurko again began pacing around beside it *with pole-axe and armour of serge*.[23] He was acquainted with the majority of the Germans who lived near the Nikitsky Gates: some of them had even had occasion to spend a Sunday night at Jurko's. He was immediately introduced to Adrian as a man of whom sooner or later he might happen to have need, and when the guests went to the table, they sat down together. Mr and Mrs Schultz and their daughter, seventeen-year-old Lottchen, dined with the guests, while all together helping them to food and assisting the cook in serving. Beer flowed. Jurko ate enough for four; Adrian did no worse than him; his daughters were on their best behaviour; the conversation in German became noisier by the minute. Suddenly the host demanded attention and, opening a tarred bottle, pronounced loudly in Russian: 'To the health of my good Louisa!' The fake champagne frothed. The host gave the fresh face of his forty-year-old helpmeet a tender kiss, and the guests drank noisily to the health of the good Louisa. 'To the health of my dear guests!' proposed the host, opening a second bottle – and the guests thanked him, draining their glasses once more. At this point, healths began to follow one after another: they drank the health of each guest individually, they drank the health of Moscow and a full dozen German towns, they drank the health of all the guilds in general and of each one in particular, they drank the health of masters and apprentices. Adrian drank with zeal and grew so merry that he himself proposed some humorous toast. Suddenly one of the guests, a fat baker, raised his glass and exclaimed: 'To the health of those we work for, *unserer Kundleute!*'[24] The proposal was, like all the others, received joyously and unanimously. The guests began bowing to one another, the tailor to the cobbler, the cobbler to the tailor, the baker to both of them, everyone to the baker, and so on. In the midst of these reciprocal bows, Jurko, addressing his neighbour, cried out: 'Well then, old fellow? Drink to the health of your dead men.' Everyone roared with laughter, but the undertaker considered himself insulted, and frowned. No one noticed it, the guests continued drinking, and the bells were already being rung for vespers when they rose from the table.

It was late when the guests dispersed, for the most part tight. The fat baker and the bookbinder, whose face

Seemed in a nice, bright-red, morocco-leather binding,[25]

led Jurko away by the arms to his sentry-box, observing in this instance the Russian proverb: one good turn deserves another. The undertaker got home drunk and cross. 'What's this, after all,' he deliberated out loud, 'in what way is my trade more dishonourable than others? Is the undertaker the brother of the executioner? What are those foreigners laughing at? Is the undertaker a pantomime clown? I'd have liked to invite them to a housewarming and give them an enormous feast: it's not going to happen, though! I'll invite those I work for instead: the Orthodox dead.' – 'What's that, sir?' said the domestic, who was taking his shoes off for him at the time, 'what's that nonsense you're talking? Cross yourself! Inviting the dead to a housewarming! What a night-mare!' – 'Honest to God, I will invite them,' Adrian continued, 'and for tomorrow. You're most welcome, my benefactors, to feast with me tomorrow evening; I'll entertain you with whatever I can.' With these words the undertaker set off to bed and soon started snoring.

It was still dark outside when Adrian was woken up. Tryukhina, the merchant's wife, had passed away that very night, and a messenger had galloped over to Adrian on horseback from her bailiff with the news. The undertaker gave him a tip of ten kopeks for doing so, got dressed in a hurry, took a cab and drove to Razgulyai. The police were already standing at the dead woman's gates, and merchants were pacing about like ravens who sense a dead body. The deceased lay on a table, yellow as wax, but not yet disfigured by decay. Around her crowded relatives, neighbours and domestics. All the windows were open; candles were burning; priests were saying prayers. Adrian went up to Tryukhina's nephew, a young merchant in a fashionable frockcoat, and declared to him that the coffin, candles, shroud and other funeral accessories would be delivered to him immediately in the very best order. The heir thanked him absentmindedly, saying that he would not haggle over the price and that he counted on his conscience in everything. The undertaker swore, as usual, that he would not overcharge; he exchanged a meaningful glance with the bailiff and drove off to get busy with things. He spent the whole day driving from Razgulyai to the Nikitsky Gates and back again; by the evening he had everything arranged and, letting his cabman go, he set off for home on foot. It was a moonlit night. The undertaker reached the Nikitsky Gates safely. By the Church of the Ascension our acquaintance Jurko hailed him and, recognising the undertaker, wished him a good night. It was late. The undertaker was already approaching his house, when suddenly it seemed to him that someone had gone up to his gates, opened the side-gate and disappeared into it. 'What could this mean?' thought Adrian. 'Who else has need of me? Could it have been a thief getting into my house? Are there lovers visiting my idiotic girls? Who knows!' And the undertaker was already thinking of calling his friend Jurko to his assistance. At that moment someone else approached the side-gate and was about to go in, but, seeing the master of the house come running up, he stopped and doffed his tricorn hat. His face seemed familiar to Adrian, but in his haste he did not have time to get a decent look at it. 'You've come to see me,' said Adrian, out of breath, 'do be so kind as to go in.' – 'Don't stand on ceremony, sir,' the other replied in muffled tones, 'go on ahead; show your guests the way!' But Adrian had no time to stand on ceremony. The gate was open, he went up the steps, and the other followed him. It seemed to Adrian that there were people walking about in his rooms. 'What devilry is this?' he thought, and hurried to go in… and at this point his legs gave way. The room was full of dead people. Coming in through the window, the moon lit their yellow and blue faces, their sunken mouths, their lacklustre, half-closed eyes and jutting noses… In horror, Adrian recognised in them people interred by his efforts, and in the guest who had come in with him the brigadier buried during the torrential rain. All of them, ladies and men, surrounded the undertaker with bows and greetings, all except one pauper, recently buried for nothing, who, abashed and ashamed of his rags, did not approach, but stood humbly in a corner. The others were all decorously dressed: the deceased ladies in bonnets and ribbons, the dead officials in uniform, but with unshaved beards, the merchants in their festive caftans. 'You see, Prokhorov,' said the brigadier in the name of the entire worthy company, 'we've all risen at your invitation: only those for whom it's already too much have stayed at home, the ones who've completely gone to pieces, and those who've only got bones left with no skin; but even then, one couldn't resist – he so wanted to pay you a visit.' At that moment a little skeleton squeezed through the crowd and went up to Adrian. His skull smiled affectionately at the undertaker. Scraps of light-green and red fabric and ancient sackcloth hung upon him here and there as if on a pole, and the bones of his legs rattled about in big jackboots like pestles in mortars. 'You don't recognise me, Prokhorov,' said the skeleton. 'Do you remember retired Guards' sergeant Pyotr Petrovich Kurilkin, the one you sold your first coffin to in 1799 – and a pine one too, making out it was oak?' With these words, the dead man opened his bony arms to him – but Adrian, summoning up his strength, cried out and pushed him away. Pyotr Petrovich tottered, fell, and completely disintegrated. Amongst the dead men there arose a murmur of indignation; they all stood up for the honour of their comrade, set upon Adrian with abuse and threats, and, deafened by their cries and almost crushed, the poor master of the house lost his presence of mind, fell down himself onto the bones of the retired Guards' sergeant, and lost consciousness.

The sun had already long been illuminating the bed on which the undertaker was lying. He finally opened his eyes and saw before him the domestic blowing the samovar into life. Adrian remembered in horror all the events of the day before. Tryukhina, the brigadier and Sergeant Kurilkin presented themselves dimly to his imagination. He waited in silence for the domestic to strike up a conversation with him and inform him of the consequences of the nocturnal adventures.

'How late you've slept, Adrian Prokhorovich, sir,' said Aksinya, handing him his dressing-gown. 'Your neighbour the tailor came to see you, and the local policeman popped in and announced that it's the police inspector's birthday today, but you were so good as to be asleep, and we didn't want to wake you up.'

'And has anyone been to see me from the late Tryukhina?'

'The late? Has she died then?'

'What a fool you are! Wasn't it you assisting me yesterday in sorting out her funeral?'

'What do you mean, sir? Have you gone barmy, or have you still not recovered from the drunken state you were in yesterday? What funeral was there yesterday? You were feasting at the German's all day long, came back drunk, fell into bed, and were asleep until this very hour, when the bells for morning mass have already stopped ringing.'

'Really?' said the gladdened undertaker.

'Of course,' replied the domestic.

'Well, if that's the case, then hurry up with the tea and call my daughters.'

THE POSTMASTER

A Registrar Collegiate,
Dictator of the posting station.

Prince Vyazemsky[26]

Who has not cursed postmasters, who has not quarrelled with them? Who, in a moment of anger, has not demanded the fateful book from them, in order to inscribe therein their useless complaint against oppression, rudeness and carelessness? Who does not consider them the scum of the earth, the equals of the scriveners of yore, or, at any rate, the Murom robbers?[27] We shall, however, be fair, we shall try to put ourselves in their position, and perhaps we shall start to judge them much more leniently. What is a postmaster? A downright martyr of the fourteenth class,[28] protected by his rank only from blows, and even then not always (I appeal to the conscience of my readers). What is the office of this dictator, as Prince Vyazemsky jokingly calls him? Is it not genuine hard labour? No peace, day or night. All the annoyance that has built up during a boring ride the traveller vents upon the postmaster. The weather is intolerable, the road is bad, the coachman is obstinate, the horses refuse to pull – and the postmaster is to blame. Entering his poor abode, the passing traveller looks upon him as an enemy; it is a good thing if he can rid himself quickly of the uninvited guest; but if there happen to be no horses?... God! What oaths, what threats rain down upon his head! In rain and slush he is obliged to run from one yard to another; in storm, in freezing cold, he goes off into the lobby just to have a minute's break from the shouting and the pushing of an irritated lodger. A general arrives; the trembling postmaster lets him have the last two troikas, including the horses meant for couriers. The general rides on without giving him a word of thanks. Five minutes later – there's a bell!... and a special messenger throws his order for horses onto the table!... If we go into it all properly, instead of indignation, our hearts will be filled with sincere compassion. A few words more: over the course of twenty years without a break I have traversed Russia in all directions; almost all of the post roads are known to me; I am acquainted with several generations of coachmen; rare is the postmaster I do not know to look at, rare is the one with whom I have had no dealings. I hope in a short time to publish my curious stock of traveller's observations; for the time being I shall only say that the estate of postmasters is presented to public opinion in the very falsest guise. These postmasters, so slandered, are generally peaceable men, obliging by nature, inclined to communal life, modest in their pretensions to honours, and not too money-grubbing. From their conversation (which passing gentlemen are wrong to scorn) much can be gleaned that is curious and instructive. As far as I am concerned, I confess I prefer their talk to the speeches of some official of the sixth class, bound somewhere on state business.

It can easily be guessed that I have friends from among the honourable estate of postmasters. Indeed, the memory of one of them is precious to me. Circumstances once brought us together, and it is of him that I now mean to talk with my gentle readers.

In 1816, in the month of May, I happened to be driving through the Province of ***, along a post road now gone. I was of minor rank, I was travelling by post-chaise and paying fares for the use of two horses. In consequence of this, postmasters did not stand on ceremony with me, and I would often take by force that which, in my opinion, was owed me by right. Being young and hot-tempered, I was indignant at the baseness and pusillanimity of the postmaster when he gave away a troika that had been prepared for me, to pull the carriage of a high-ranking gentleman. It took just as long for me to manage to get used to a discriminating lackey failing to serve me a dish at a governor's dinner-table. Nowadays, the one and the other seem to me in the order of things. What, indeed, would become of us, if, instead of the universally convenient rule: *rank respect rank*, another were brought into use, for example, *intelligence respect intelligence*? What arguments would arise! And with whom would the servants start serving the food? But I turn to my tale.

The day was hot. Three kilometres from the station of *** it began to spit, and a minute later, torrential rain had soaked me to the skin. On arrival at the station, my first concern was to get changed as quickly as possible, my second to order myself some tea. 'Hey, Dunya!' cried the postmaster, 'put the samovar on and go and get some cream.' At these words, out from behind the partition came a girl of about fourteen, who ran into the lobby. I was struck by her beauty. 'Is that your daughter?' I asked the postmaster. 'It is, sir,' he replied with an air of contented self-esteem, 'and she's so clever, so quick, she's just like her late mother.' At that point he set about copying out my order for post-horses, and I occupied myself examining the pictures that decorated his humble but tidy abode. They depicted the story of the prodigal son: in the first, a venerable old man in a cap and housecoat is releasing a restless youth, who hurriedly accepts his blessing and a bag of money. Depicted in vivid outlines in another is the young man's dissipated behaviour: he sits at a table, surrounded by false friends and shameless women. Further on, having squandered his money, the youth, in rags and a tricorn hat, is tending pigs and sharing his meal with them; depicted in his face are deep sadness and repentance. Represented finally is his return to his father; the kind old man in the same cap and housecoat is running out to meet him: the prodigal son is on his knees; in the background the cook is killing the fatted calf, and the elder brother is questioning the servants about the reason for such joy. Underneath each picture I read seemly German verses. It is all preserved in my memory to this day, just as are the pots of balsam, and the bed with the brightly coloured curtain and the other objects surrounding me at the time. I can see, as if it were now, the master himself, a man of about fifty, fresh, hale and hearty, and his long, green frockcoat with three medals on faded ribbons.

I had not had time to settle up with my old coachman before Dunya returned with the samovar. The little coquette noticed at second glance the impression she had made on me; she lowered her big, blue eyes; I started talking to her, and she answered me without any shyness, like a girl who had seen society. I offered her father a glass of punch; I gave Dunya a cup of tea, and the three of us began talking as though we had known one another for ages.

The horses had long been ready, but still I did not want to part with the postmaster and his daughter. Finally I bid them farewell; the father wished me a good journey, and the daughter accompanied me as far as the wagon. In the lobby I paused and asked her permission to kiss her; Dunya consented. Many kisses can I number,

Since first I started to enjoy them,[29]

but not one has left me with such a pleasant memory for such a long time.

Several years passed, and circumstances brought me onto that very road, to those very parts. I recalled the daughter of the old postmaster and rejoiced at the idea of seeing her again. But, I thought, perhaps the old postmaster had already been replaced; Dunya was probably already married. The idea of the death of one or the other flashed through my mind as well, and I approached the station of *** with sad foreboding.

The horses stopped by the postmaster's little house. Entering the room, I recognised at once the pictures showing the story of the prodigal son; the table and bed stood in their former places; but there were no longer any flowers on the windowsills, and all around displayed dilapidation and neglect. The postmaster was asleep beneath a sheepskin coat; my arrival woke him; he half rose... It was definitely Samson Virin; but how he had aged! While he was preparing to copy out my order for horses, I looked at his grey hair, at the deep wrinkles on the long unshaven face, at the bent back – and could not cease to wonder at how three or four years could have turned a hale and hearty man into an old, decrepit one. 'Do you recognise me?' I asked him, 'you and I are old acquaintances.' – 'It may well be so,' he answered gloomily, 'this here's a major road, and I've had a lot of travellers here.' – 'Is your Dunya well?' I continued. The old man frowned. 'God knows,' he replied. 'She's evidently married, then?' I said. The old man pretended he had not heard my question and continued reading my order in a whisper. I ceased my questions and bid him put the kettle on. Curiosity was starting to niggle me, and I hoped that some punch would loosen my old acquaintance's tongue.

I was not mistaken: the old man did not refuse the glass he was offered. I noticed that the rum brightened up his gloom. On the second glass he became talkative: he remembered, or put on an appearance of remembering me, and I heard from him a tale which interested and touched me greatly at the time.

'So you knew my Dunya?' he began. 'And who didn't know her? Ah, Dunya, Dunya! What a lass she was! Whoever was passing through, they all used to praise her, no one would criticise. The ladies would give her presents, one a headscarf, another earrings. Passing gentlemen used to stop on purpose, as if to have dinner or supper, but really just to gaze at her for a little bit longer. However cross a gentleman was, he used to calm down when she was there and talk to me politely. Can you believe it, sir: couriers and special messengers used to end up talking to her for half an hour at a time. She held the house together: tidying here, cooking there, she managed it all. And I, old fool that I was, I couldn't look at her enough, couldn't dote on her enough; did I not love my Dunya, did I not cherish my little child; did she not have a good life? No, prayers won't help you escape misfortune; what's fated to be, can't be avoided.' And here he began telling me in detail about his woe. – One winter's evening three years before, when the postmaster was ruling lines in a new book and his daughter was behind the partition, making herself a dress, a troika drove up, and a traveller in a Circassian hat and a military greatcoat, all wrapped up in a shawl, entered the room demanding horses. The horses were all out. At this news the traveller was about to raise his voice and his whip; but Dunya, who was used to such scenes, ran out from behind the partition and addressed the traveller amiably with a question as to whether he would like anything to eat. Dunya's appearance had its usual effect. The traveller's anger passed; he agreed to wait for horses and ordered himself supper. On removing his wet, shaggy hat, disentangling the shawl and pulling off the greatcoat, the traveller proved to be a young, slim hussar with a little black moustache. He made himself comfortable in the postmaster's house and began talking cheerfully to him and his daughter. Supper was served. In the meantime, horses had arrived, and the postmaster had ordered them to be harnessed to the traveller's kibitka at once, without being fed; but on returning, he found the young man lying on a bench almost unconscious: he'd had a bad turn, his head had started aching, he couldn't travel… What was to be done! The postmaster gave up his bed to him, and it was proposed, if the sick man was no better, to send to S*** the next morning for the doctor.

The next day, the hussar was worse. His man rode into town for the doctor. Dunya tied a headscarf soaked in vinegar around his head and sat down with her sewing by his bed. In front of the postmaster the sick man groaned and hardly said a word, yet he did drink two cups of coffee and, groaning, ordered himself dinner. Dunya never left his side. He was continually asking for something to drink, and Dunya would help him with the mug of lemonade she had prepared. The sick man would moisten his lips, and every time he returned the mug, he gave Dunyushka's hand a squeeze with his own weak one to signify his gratitude. Towards dinnertime the doctor arrived. He felt the sick man's pulse, had a word with him in German, and announced in Russian that he only needed peace and quiet, and that in a couple of days he would be able to set off on his journey. The hussar handed him twenty-five roubles for his visit and invited him to have dinner; the doctor accepted; both ate with great appetite, they finished a bottle of wine and parted very pleased with each other.

Another day passed and the hussar was completely recovered. He was extremely cheerful and joked incessantly, now with Dunya, now with the postmaster; he whistled songs, talked to travellers, entered their orders for horses in the post book, and made the kind postmaster so fond of him that on the third morning he felt sorry to part with his amiable lodger. It was a Sunday; Dunya was preparing to go to morning mass. The hussar's kibitka was made ready. He bade the postmaster farewell, rewarding him generously for the board and lodging; he bade farewell to Dunya too, and volunteered to take her with him as far as the church, which was situated on the outskirts of the village. Dunya stood in a quandary… 'What are you afraid of?' her father said to her, 'his Honour isn't a wolf and won't eat you, will he: go on and have a ride as far as the church.' Dunya got into the kibitka next to the hussar, his servant leapt up onto the coachman's seat, the coachman whistled and the horses set off at a gallop.

The poor postmaster did not understand how he himself could have allowed his Dunya to go with the hussar, how he had come to be so blind, and what had been the matter with his mind then. Not half an hour had passed before his heart began to ache and ache, and disquiet took hold of him to such a degree that he could not restrain himself and went off to morning mass himself. Approaching the church, he saw that the people were already dispersing, but Dunya was neither within the fence, nor in the porch. He hurriedly entered the church: the priest was coming out from the altar; the sexton was snuffing out the candles, and two old women were still praying in a corner; but Dunya was not inside the church. Only with an effort did the poor father resolve to ask the sexton whether she had been at mass. The sexton replied that she had not. The postmaster went home more dead than alive. One hope remained to him: with the frivolity of youth, Dunya had perhaps taken it into her head to ride as far as the next station, where her godmother lived. In agonising agitation he awaited the return of the troika with which he had let her go. The coachman did not return. Finally, towards evening, he arrived, alone and tipsy, with deadly news: 'Dunya went on from that station with the hussar.'

The old man could not bear his misfortune; he took straight away to that very bed where the young deceiver had lain the day before. Now, considering all the circumstances, the postmaster guessed that the sickness had been feigned. The poor man fell ill with a high fever; he was taken to S***, and another man was appointed temporarily to his position. The same doctor who had come to the hussar treated him too. He assured the postmaster that the young man had been perfectly well, and that even at the time he had guessed at his malicious intention, but had kept quiet, fearing his whip. Whether the German was telling the truth, or only wished to boast of his far-sightedness, his words did not comfort the poor sick man in the least. Barely had the postmaster recovered from his illness before he begged two months' leave of his superior in S*** and, without saying a word to anyone about his intention, set off on foot after his daughter. From his order for horses he knew that Captain Minsky had been travelling from Smolensk to St Petersburg. The coachman who had driven him said Dunya had cried all the way, although she had seemed to be going of her own accord. 'Maybe,' thought the postmaster, 'I'll bring my lost sheep home.' With this idea he arrived in St Petersburg, put up in the Izmailov Regiment quarter, at the home of a retired corporal, his old comrade-in-arms, and began his search. He soon learnt that Captain Minsky was in St Petersburg and staying at the Demutov Inn. The postmaster resolved to pay him a visit.

Early in the morning he arrived in his entrance hall and requested that his Honour be told that an old soldier was asking to see him. The military servant, cleaning a boot on a boot-tree, declared that the master was asleep and that he received no one before eleven o'clock. The postmaster went away, and returned at the appointed time. Minsky himself came out to him, wearing his dressing gown and a red skullcap. 'What is it you want, brother?' he asked him. The old man's heart began to seethe, tears welled up in his eyes, and in a tremulous voice he pronounced only: 'Your Honour!... For the love of God, please!...' Minsky threw a quick glance at him, flushed, took him by the arm, led him into the study and closed the door behind him. 'Your Honour!' the old man continued, 'it's no use crying over spilt milk: but at least give me back my poor Dunya. You've had your fun with her, haven't you? Don't go and ruin her for no reason.' – 'What's done can't be undone,' said the young man in extreme embarrassment, 'I'm at fault before you and gladly ask your forgiveness; but don't think that I might abandon Dunya: she will be happy, I give you my word of honour. What do you want her for? She loves me; her former status would be strange to her now. Neither you, nor she will forget what has happened.' Then, tucking something into the postmaster's cuff, he opened the door, and, with no recollection of how, the postmaster found himself out in the street.

He stood motionless for a long time, but finally saw a bundle of papers inside the cuff of his sleeve; he took them out, and unfolded several crumpled five- and ten-rouble banknotes. Tears welled up in his eyes again, tears of indignation! He squeezed the notes into a ball, threw them onto the ground, trampled them down with his heel and set off... After moving several paces away, he stopped, had a think... and turned back... but the banknotes were no longer there. Seeing the postmaster, a well-dressed young man ran up to a cab, hurriedly got in and cried: 'Drive on!...' The postmaster did not pursue him. He resolved to set off home to his station, but first he wanted to see his poor Dunya just one more time. To this end, he returned to Minsky's a day or two later; but the military servant said to him sternly that the master was receiving no one, he forced him out of the hall with his chest and slammed the door right in his face. The postmaster stood and stood – and then went away.

That same day, in the evening, he was walking along Liteiny after going to a service at All Sorrows. Suddenly a smart droshky sped by in front of him, and the postmaster recognised Minsky. The droshky stopped in front of a three-storeyed house, right by the entrance, and the hussar ran up into the porch. A happy thought flashed through the postmaster's head. He turned back and, drawing level with the coachman, asked: 'Whose is this horse, brother? Is it Minsky's?' – 'It certainly is,' answered the coachman, 'and what's it to you?' – 'It's this: your master ordered me to take a note to his Dunya, and I've gone and forgotten where his Dunya lives.' – 'Right here, on the first floor. But you're too late with your note, brother; he's with her himself now.' – 'Never mind,' the postmaster retorted with an inexpressible stirring in his heart, 'thanks for the advice, but I'll finish my job.' And with these words he went up the steps.

The doors were locked; he rang the bell, and spent several seconds in painful expectation. There was the clatter of the key, and the door was opened. 'Is Avdotya Samsonovna staying here?' he asked. 'Yes,' replied the young housemaid, 'and what do you want with her?' Without answering, the postmaster went into the reception hall. 'You can't, you can't!' the housemaid cried in his wake, 'Avdotya Samsonovna has guests.' But the postmaster carried on without listening. The first two rooms were dark; in the third there was a light. He went up to the open door and stopped. In the beautifully decorated room sat Minsky, deep in thought. Dunya, dressed in all the splendour of high fashion, was sitting on the arm of his chair like a horsewoman riding side saddle the English way. She was looking at Minsky tenderly, and winding his black curls round her glittering fingers. The poor postmaster! Never had his daughter seemed to him so beautiful; involuntarily he feasted his eyes upon her. 'Who's there?' she asked, without raising her head. He remained silent. Receiving no reply, Dunya did raise her head... and fell with a cry onto the rug. In fright, Minsky rushed to help her up, then, suddenly seeing the old postmaster in the doorway, he left Dunya and went up to him, trembling with rage. 'What do you want?' he said to him, clenching his teeth, 'why are you stealing after me everywhere, like a robber? Or do you want to murder me? Get out!' And seizing the old man by the collar, he pushed him with a strong hand out onto the steps.

The old man arrived at his quarters. His friend advised him to make a complaint; but the postmaster thought about it, waved his hand and resolved to give it up. Two days later he set off from St Petersburg back to his station and took up his duties once again. 'It's more than two years now,' he concluded, 'that I've been living without Dunya and haven't heard a single word about her. God knows whether she's alive or not. Anything might happen. She's not the first, and not the last to be lured away by a passing rake, who's kept her for a bit and then dumped her. There are lots of them in St Petersburg, silly young girls, in satin and velvet one day, and the next, look at them, they're sweeping the street along with the riff-raff from the tavern. Sometimes when you think Dunya may be wasting away there too, you can't help but be sinful and wish her in the grave...'

Such was the story of my friend, the old postmaster, a story interrupted more than once by tears, which he wiped away in picturesque fashion with his coat tail, like the zealous Terentyich in Dmitriyev's fine ballad.[30] Those tears were aroused in part by the punch, of which he knocked back five glasses in the course of his narrative; but however that might be, they touched my heart deeply. For a long time after parting with him I could not forget the old postmaster, for a long time I thought of poor Dunya...

Only recently, passing through the little town of ***, I remembered my friend; I learnt that the station of which he had been in charge had already gone. To my question: 'Is the old postmaster alive?' no one could give me a satisfactory answer. I resolved to visit the familiar spot, took private horses and set out for the village of N.

This was in the autumn. Little grey clouds were covering the sky, a cold wind was blowing from the harvested fields, carrying red and yellow leaves off from the trees with which it met. I arrived in the village at the setting of the sun and stopped by the post-house. A fat peasant woman came out into the lobby (where once poor Dunya had kissed me), and to my questions replied that the old postmaster had been dead about a year, that a brewer had moved into his house, and that she was the brewer's wife. I began to regret my journey, made in vain, and the seven roubles expended for nothing. 'What did he die of?' I asked the brewer's wife. 'He drank himself to death, sir,' she replied. 'And where is he buried?' – 'Outside the village, next to his late missus.' – 'I couldn't be taken to his grave, could I?' – 'Why ever not? Hey, Vanka! That's quite enough playing with the cat. You take the gentleman to the grave-yard and point out the postmaster's grave to him.'

At these words a ragged boy ran out to me, ginger-haired and blind in one eye, and immediately led me out of the village.

'Did you know the dead man?' I asked him on the way.

'Of course I did! He taught me how to carve whistles. There were times he'd be leaving the tavern (God rest his soul!), and we'd be going along after him: "Granddad, granddad! Give us some nuts!" And he'd treat us to some nuts. He was always playing with us.'

'And do passing travellers remember him?'

'There aren't many travellers nowadays; there's only the magistrate might turn up, and he's got no interest in the dead. Now in the summer there was a lady passing through, and she asked about the old post master, and she visited his grave.'

'What sort of lady?' I asked with curiosity.

'A beautiful lady,' the little boy replied; 'she was riding in a six-horse carriage with three young masters and a wet-nurse, and with a black pug dog; and when she was told the old postmaster was dead, she burst out crying and said to the children: "Sit quietly, and I'll go to the grave-yard." And I was about to volunteer to take her. But the lady said: "I know the way myself." And she gave me a silver five-kopek piece – such a kind lady!…'

We arrived at the graveyard, a bare place, not fenced in at all, sown with wooden crosses, unshielded by a single little tree. In all my days I had not seen such a mournful graveyard.

'Here's the old postmaster's grave,' the boy said to me, jumping up onto a pile of sand into which had been planted a black cross with a copper icon.

'And the lady came here?' I asked.

'She did,' Vanka replied, 'I watched her from a distance. She lay down here, and stayed lying down for a long time. And then the lady went into the village and called for the priest, gave him some money and drove away, and she gave me a silver five-kopek piece – a lovely lady!'

I gave the little boy five kopeks too, and no longer regretted either the journey, or the seven roubles I had spent.

MISTRESS PEASANT

In any costume, Dushenka, you're beautiful.

Bogdanovich[31]

In one of our remote provinces lay the estate of Ivan Petrovich Berestov. In his youth he served in the Guards, he resigned his commission at the beginning of 1797, went away to his village and thereafter never left it. He was married to a poor noblewoman who died in childbirth while he was out hunting far from home. Exercises in husbandry soon consoled him. He built a house to his own design, set up his own cloth mill, tripled his income and began to consider himself the cleverest man in the entire area, something in which the neighbours who came to stay with their families and dogs did not gainsay him. On ordinary days he went about in a velveteen jacket, on holidays he put on a frockcoat of home-made cloth; he himself kept a record of expenditure, and he read nothing except for *The Senate Gazette*. He was generally liked, albeit considered proud. The only person who did not get on with him was Grigory Ivanovich Muromsky, his nearest neighbour. He was a true member of the Russian landowning gentry. Having squandered the greater part of his estate in Moscow and become by that time a widower, he went away to his last remaining village, where he continued to get up to mischief, but already of a new kind. He laid out an English garden, on which he spent almost all of his remaining income. His grooms were dressed as English jockeys. His daughter had an English governess. He worked his fields according to the English method:

But Russian crops won't grow, worked in a foreign manner,[32]

and despite a significant reduction in expenditure, Grigory Ivanovich's income did not increase; even in the countryside he found a way of getting into new debt; he was, withal, considered a man not stupid, for he was the first landowner of his province to have the sense to mortgage his estate with the Board of Trustees,[33] a move which at the time seemed extremely complex and bold. Of those who censured him, it was Berestov who expressed his opinion most sternly of all. Hatred of innovation was a distinctive feature of his character. He was unable to speak with indifference of the Anglomania of his neighbour and was continually finding opportunities to criticise him. If he was showing a guest his domain, in reply to praise for his farming arrangements he would say with a sly grin: 'Oh, yes! But what I have here can't compare with what my neighbour Grigory Ivanovich has. How could we possibly go broke the English way! We can only hope to be well fed the Russian way.' Thanks to the zeal of neighbours, these and similar jokes were brought to the attention of Grigory Ivanovich, together with additional material and explanations. The Anglomaniac bore criticism just as impatiently as our Russian journalists do. He was furious, and called his Zoilus[34] a bear and a provincial.

Such were the relations between these two property owners when Berestov's son came out to the country to visit him. He had been educated at the University of *** and was intending to enter military service, but his father would not agree to it. The young man felt himself quite incapable of civilian service. They refused to yield to one another, and in the meantime young Alexei started living as a country gentleman and letting his moustache grow, just in case.

Alexei really was a fine young fellow. It would truly be a shame if his slim figure were never squeezed into a military uniform and if, instead of cutting a dash on a steed, he spent his youth bent over official papers. Looking at the way he was always galloping in the forefront of the hunt while paying no heed to the route, the neighbours were in accord that he would never make a sensible head of section. The young ladies threw glances at him, and some simply could not take their eyes off him; yet Alexei was concerned with them but little, and they supposed an amorous liaison to be the reason for his insensitivity. Indeed, a copy of the address on one of his letters was passed from hand to hand: *to Akulina Petrovna Kurochkina, in Moscow, opposite the St Alexei Monastery, in the house of the coppersmith Savelyev, and you I humbly request to deliver this letter to A.N.R.*

Those of my readers who have never lived in the country cannot imagine what a delight those provincial young ladies are! Brought up on fresh air, in the shade of the apple trees in their orchards, they glean their knowledge of the world and life from books. Solitude, freedom and reading early develop in them feelings and passions unknown to our distracted beauties. For a provincial young lady the ringing of a harness-bell is already an adventure, a trip to a nearby town is considered an epoch in life, and the visit of a guest leaves a long-lasting, sometimes even eternal memory. Of course, anyone is free to laugh at some of their oddities, but the jokes of a superficial observer cannot destroy their essential virtues, the chief of which is *peculiarity of character, originality (individualité)*, without which, in the opinion of Jean-Paul,[35] neither can human greatness exist. Perhaps in the capitals women receive a better education; but experience of society soon smoothes out character and makes souls just as monotonous as hats. Let this be said not in judgement, and not in censure, but nonetheless: *Nota nostra manet*,[36] as one ancient commentator writes.

It is easy to imagine what an impression Alexei must have made in the circle of our young ladies. He was the first to appear before them gloomy and disenchanted, the first to speak to them of lost joys and his faded youth; moreover, he wore a black ring with the image of a death's head. This was all extremely new in this province. The young ladies went mad over him.

But more interested in him than anyone was the daughter of my Anglomaniac, Liza (or Betsy, as Grigory Ivanovich usually called her). The fathers did not call on one another, and she had not yet seen Alexei, while all her young female neighbours talked of nothing but him. She was seventeen. Black eyes animated her dark-complexioned and very pleasant face. She was an only, and consequently spoilt child. Her playfulness and continual mischief were the delight of her father and the despair of her governess, Miss Jackson, a prim spinster of forty who powdered her face and put kohl on her eyebrows, reread *Pamela*[37] twice a year, was paid two thousand roubles for doing so, and was dying of boredom 'in this barbarous Russia'.

Liza was attended by Nastya; she was a little older, but just as frivolous as her mistress was. Liza was very fond of her, disclosed all her secrets to her, considered her escapades together with her; in short, Nastya was a much more significant figure in the village of Priluchino than any confidante in a French tragedy.

'May I go visiting today?' said Nastya one day, as she was dressing her mistress.

'Certainly; where?'

'Tugilovo, the Berestovs'. It's their cook's wife's birthday, and yesterday she came and invited us to dinner.'

'There!' said Liza, 'the masters have fallen out, but the servants are entertaining one another.'

'What do we care about our masters!' Nastya retorted, 'what's more, I'm yours, not your Papa's. You haven't quarrelled with young Berestov yet, have you; just let the old men fight, if they enjoy it.'

'Try and get a glimpse of Alexei Berestov, Nastya, and give me a thorough account of what he looks like and what sort of man he is.'

Nastya promised, and Liza waited impatiently the whole day for her return. In the evening Nastya appeared. 'Well, Lizaveta Grigoryevna,' she said, coming into the room, 'I've seen young Berestov; I've had a pretty good look; we were together the whole day.'

'How did that happen? Tell me, tell me right from the beginning.'

'Certainly, miss: off we went, me, Anisya Yegorovna, Nenila, Dunka…'

'All right, I know. Well, and then?'

'Let me tell you everything right from the beginning, miss. So, we arrived just in time for dinner. The room was full of people. The Kholbins' people were there, the Zakharevs', the steward's wife with her daughters, the Khlupins'…'

'But what about Berestov?'

'Wait, miss. So we sat down at the table, the steward's wife in the place of honour, me next to her… and her daughters went into a sulk, but I couldn't care less about them…'

'Oh Nastya, how boring you are with your eternal details!'

'And how impatient you are! Well, so we got up from the table… we'd been sitting for about three hours, and the dinner was splendid; blue, red and striped blancmange tarts… So we got up from the table and went into the garden to play catch, and it was then that the young gentleman appeared.'

'Well then? Is it true that he's so good-looking?'

'Amazingly good-looking, handsome, you might say. Slim, tall, rosy cheeks…'

'Really? And I'd been thinking he had a pale face. Well? How did he seem to you? Sad, pensive?'

'What do you mean? I've never seen such a wild one in all my life. He took it into his head to run around playing catch with us.'

'Playing catch with you? Impossible!'

'Perfectly possible! And that's not all he thought of! He'd catch you and then start kissing you!'

'Say what you will, Nastya, you're lying.'

'Say what you will, I'm not. It was all I could do to get rid of him. He spent the whole day messing about with us like that.'

'But how can it be, they say he's in love and doesn't look at anyone?'

'I don't know, miss, but he looked at me a bit too much, and at Tanya, the steward's daughter, too; and at the Kholbins' Pasha, and I'm afraid to say he didn't leave anyone neglected, such a scamp!'

'This is amazing! And what's to be heard about him in the house?'

'A fine gentleman, they say: so kind, so cheerful. The one bad thing is that he's too fond of chasing after girls. But that doesn't matter, in my view: he'll settle down with time.'

'How I'd like to see him!' said Liza with a sigh.

'And what's so difficult about that? Tugilovo's not far from us, only three kilometres: go and take a walk in that direction, or go on horseback; you're sure to meet him. He goes out hunting with his gun every day, early in the morning.'

'No, that would be wrong. He might think I was chasing after him. What's more, our fathers have fallen out, and so I won't be able to make his acquaintance anyway… Oh, Nastya! Do you know what? I'll dress up as a peasant!'

'Quite right; put on a thick blouse, a sarafan, and step out boldly for Tugilovo; Berestov won't let you slip by, I guarantee.'

'And I'm really good at talking the way they do around here. Oh Nastya, dear Nastya! What a splendid idea!' And Liza went to bed with the firm intention of executing her light-hearted design.

The very next day, she set about the execution of her plan; she sent someone to buy some thick linen, blue nankeen and brass buttons at the market, with Nastya's help she cut out a blouse and sarafan for herself, she set the whole of the maids' room to work sewing, and by the evening everything was ready. Liza tried her new clothes on and acknowledged in front of the mirror that she had never before seemed so pretty to herself. She rehearsed her role, bowing low as she walked and then shaking her head several times in the manner of a clay cat, she spoke in the peasant dialect, laughed while hiding her face with her sleeve, and earned Nastya's complete approval. One thing gave her difficulty: she was going to try and walk across the yard bare-footed, but the turf pricked her delicate feet, and the sand and little stones seemed unbearable to her. Nastya helped her here too: she took down the measurements of Liza's foot, ran into the fields to Trofim the shepherd and ordered a pair of bast shoes of that size from him. At an unearthly hour the next day, Liza was already awake. The whole house was still asleep. Nastya was outside the gates waiting for the shepherd. A horn began to blow, and the village flock stretched out past the master's yard. As he went by in front of Nastya, Trofim handed her a pair of small, brightly coloured bast shoes and received fifty kopeks from her in reward. Liza quietly dressed herself up as a peasant, in a whisper gave Nastya her instructions concerning Miss Jackson, went out onto the rear porch, and ran through the kitchen garden into the fields.

The dawn was shining in the east, and golden lines of clouds seemed to be waiting for the sun, the way courtiers await the sovereign; the clear sky, the morning freshness, the dew, the breeze and the singing of the birds filled Liza's heart with the gaiety of an infant; afraid of meeting someone she knew, she seemed not to walk, but to fly. Approaching the grove that stood on the boundary of her father's domain, Liza began moving more gently. Here she was to wait for Alexei. Her heart was beating hard, without itself knowing why; but the fear that accompanies our youthful mischief comprises its chief delight too. Liza entered the twilight of the grove. Its muffled waves of sound greeted the girl. Her gaiety abated. Little by little she gave herself up to sweet dreaminess. She thought… but is it possible to determine with precision what a young miss of seventeen is thinking about, alone, in a grove, before six o'clock on a spring morning? And so she was walking, deep in thought, along the road, shielded on both sides by tall trees, when suddenly a splendid pointer began barking at her. Liza took fright and cried out. At the same time a voice rang out: '*Tout beau, Sbogar, ici…*'[38] and a young huntsman appeared from behind some bushes. 'Don't be afraid, dear,' he said to Liza, 'my dog doesn't bite.' Liza had already managed to recover from her fright and was able to exploit the circumstances straight away. 'No, master,' she said, pretending to be half-frightened, half-shy, 'I am afraid: see how vicious it is; it may launch itself again.' Alexei (the reader will already have recognised him) was in the meantime gazing intently at the young peasant girl. 'I'll walk with you, if you're afraid,' he said to her; 'will you permit me to walk beside you?' – 'Who's stopping you, then?' replied Liza, 'you can suit yourself, and it's a public road.' – 'Where are you from?' – 'Priluchino; I'm Vasily the blacksmith's daughter, out picking mushrooms.' (Liza was carrying a little basket on a string.) 'And you, master? From Tugilovo are you?' – 'Exactly,' replied Alexei, 'I'm the young master's valet.' Alexei wanted to make their relationship one of equals. But Liza looked at him and laughed. 'You're lying, though,' she said, 'you've not come upon an idiot. I can see you're the master himself.' – 'And what makes you think that?' – 'Everything.' – 'But really?' – 'How can you fail to tell the difference between a master and a servant? You're dressed wrong, and you talk a different way, and you call your dog in some other language.' With every minute, Alexei liked Liza more. He was not used to standing on ceremony with pretty girls from the village and was about to try and put his arm around her; but Liza jumped back away from him and suddenly adopted such a stern and cold air that, although it made Alexei laugh, still it deterred him from further attempts. 'If you want us to be friends in the future,' she said pompously, 'be so good as not to forget yourself.' – 'Who taught you such wisdom?' asked Alexei, roaring with laughter. 'Not my acquaintance Nastyenka, was it, not your mistress' maid? So those are the ways enlightenment gets spread!' Liza sensed that she was on the point of leaving her role, and corrected herself at once. 'What do you think, then?' she said, 'don't I ever go to the master's house? Don't you worry: I've heard and seen my share of all sorts of things. Still,' she continued, 'I won't get any mushrooms collected, chattering with you. You go one way, master, and I'll go the other. Begging your pardon…' Liza wanted to move away, but Alexei detained her by the hand. 'What's your name, my dear?' – 'Akulina,' answered Liza, trying to free her fingers from Alexei's hand; 'now let me go, sir; it's time I went home too.' – 'Well, Akulina my friend, I'll be sure to come and visit your father, Vasily the blacksmith.' – 'What do you mean?' objected Liza animatedly, 'for Christ's sake, don't. If they find out at home that I've been chattering with a gentleman in the grove on my own, I'll be in trouble; my father, Vasily the blacksmith, he'll beat me to death.' – 'But I want to see you again, without fail.' – 'Well, I'll come here for mushrooms again some time.' – 'When?' – 'Maybe even tomorrow.' – 'Dear Akulina, I'd smother you with kisses, only I don't dare. Tomorrow, then, at this time, is that right?' – 'Yes, yes.' – 'And you won't deceive me?' – 'No, I won't.' – 'Swear to it.' – 'I swear by Good Friday, I'll come.'

The youngsters parted. Liza emerged from the wood, crossed the field, stole into the garden and ran headlong to the farm, where Nastya was waiting for her. There she changed her clothes, giving absent-minded answers to her impatient confidante's questions, and went into the drawing room. The table was laid, breakfast was ready, and Miss Jackson, already powdered and squeezed into a wasp waist, was cutting thin slices of bread and butter. Her father praised her for her early walk. 'There's nothing healthier,' he said, 'than waking up at dawn.' Here he gave several examples, drawn from English journals, of long life in humans, remarking that everyone who lived for more than a hundred years abstained from vodka and rose at dawn in winter and summer. Liza did not listen to him. She was repeating in her thoughts all the circumstances of the morning's meeting, the whole of Akulina's conversation with the young huntsman, and her conscience was starting to trouble her. In vain did she object to herself that their conversation had not gone beyond the bounds of decorum, that this prank could not have any consequences: her conscience murmured louder than her reason. The promise she had given for the following day worried her most of all: she was quite on the point of making up her mind not to keep her solemn oath. But after waiting for her in vain, Alexei might go looking in the village for the real Akulina, the daughter of Vasily the blacksmith, a fat, pock-marked girl, and thus guess at her frivolous mischief. This idea horrified Liza, and she made up her mind to go to the grove again the next morning as Akulina.

For his part, Alexei was in raptures, and he spent the whole day thinking about his new acquaintance; in the night, the image of the dark beauty haunted his imagination even in his dreams. Day was barely breaking, and he was already dressed. Without allowing himself the time to load his rifle, he went out into the fields with his faithful Sbogar and ran off to the place of the promised meeting. Some half an hour passed in anticipation that he found intolerable; suddenly he caught a glimpse of a blue sarafan between the bushes and rushed to meet his dear Akulina. She smiled at the rapture of his gratitude; but Alexei noticed traces of dejection and disquiet on her face at once. He wanted to know the reason for it. Liza confessed that her action seemed to her frivolous, that she repented of it, that this time she had not wanted to fail to keep the word she had given, but that this meeting would already be the last, and she asked him to cut short an acquaintance which could not lead to anything good. It was all said, it stands to reason, in the peasant dialect; but the thoughts and feelings, unusual in a simple girl, astonished Alexei. He employed all his eloquence to deflect her from her intention; he assured her of the innocence of his desires, promised never to give her grounds for repentance, to obey her in everything, entreated her not to deprive him of his one joy: seeing her alone, if only every other day, if only twice a week. He spoke in the language of true passion, and at that moment he was definitely in love. Liza listened to him in silence. 'Give me your word,' she said at last, 'that you'll never look for me in the village or ask questions about me. Give me your word not to seek any meetings with me besides the ones I fix myself.' Alexei was about to swear to her by Good Friday, but she stopped him with a smile. 'I don't need an oath,' said Liza, 'your promise alone is enough.' After that they talked amicably, strolling together through the wood, until Liza told him it was time. They parted, and Alexei, remaining alone, could not understand how a simple country girl had managed in two meetings to acquire real power over him. His relations with Akulina had the charm of novelty for him, and although the strange peasant girl's injunctions seemed to him onerous, still the idea of not keeping his word did not even occur to him. The fact of the matter was that Alexei, despite the fateful ring, the mysterious correspondence and the gloomy disenchantment, was a good and ardent fellow and had a pure heart, capable of enjoying the pleasures of innocence.

If I were to obey my own inclination alone, I would be sure to set about describing the youngsters' meetings in every detail, their increasing mutual disposition and trustfulness, their doings, conversations; but I know that the greater part of my readers would not share my pleasure with me. Those details must in general seem sickly sweet, and so I shall omit them, saying in brief that not even two months had yet passed before my Alexei was already head over heels in love, and Liza was not indifferent, albeit more taciturn than he. They were both happy with the present and thought little about the future.

The idea of indissoluble ties flashed through their minds quite frequently, but never did they talk about this with each other. The reason is obvious: however attached he was to his dear Akulina, Alexei always remembered the distance that existed between him and the poor peasant girl; and Liza knew the hatred that existed between their fathers, and did not dare to hope for a mutual reconciliation. Moreover, her self-esteem was secretly excited by the dark, romantic hope of finally seeing the Tugilovo landowner at the feet of the daughter of the Priluchino blacksmith. Then suddenly an important occurrence all but altered their mutual relations.

One clear, cold morning (one of those in which our Russian autumn is rich), Ivan Petrovich Berestov went out for a ride on horseback, taking with him in case of need two or three pairs of borzoi hounds, a groom and a number of serf boys with rattles. At the same time, Grigory Ivanovich Muromsky, tempted by the good weather, ordered his bob-tailed mare to be saddled and set off at a trot around his anglicised domain. Riding towards the wood, he caught sight of his neighbour sitting proudly on his horse in a cloth jacket lined with fox-fur and waiting for the hare which the boys were driving out of the bushes with their cries and rattles. If Grigory Ivanovich could have foreseen this meeting, he would, of course, have turned aside; but he had come upon Berestov quite unexpectedly, and suddenly found himself the distance of a pistol shot away from him. There was nothing for it. Muromsky, as an educated European, rode up to his adversary and greeted him courteously. Berestov replied with the same zeal with which, at its handler's bidding, a chained bear bows 'to the gentlemen'. At this point the hare leapt out of the wood and ran off across the field. Berestov and the groom shouted at the tops of their voices, released the dogs and galloped off after them at top speed. Muromsky's horse, which had never been out hunting, took fright and bolted. Muromsky, who had proclaimed himself an excellent horseman, gave it free rein, and was inwardly pleased at the chance which had delivered him from an unpleasant interlocutor. But the horse, reaching a gully it had not previously noticed, suddenly flung itself to one side, and Muromsky failed to keep his seat. Falling quite heavily on the frozen earth, he lay cursing his bob-tailed mare, which, as though having come to its senses, had stopped at once as soon as it felt itself riderless. Ivan Petrovich galloped up to him, enquiring whether he was injured. The groom, meanwhile, led up the guilty horse, holding it by the bridle. He helped Muromsky to clamber up into the saddle, and Berestov invited him home. Muromsky could not refuse, for he felt himself obliged, and Berestov thus returned home in glory, having hunted down the hare, and leading his wounded adversary almost as a prisoner of war.

While having breakfast, the neighbours got into quite friendly conversation. Muromsky asked Berestov for his droshky, as he acknowledged that because of the injury he was in no condition to ride home on horseback. Berestov saw him out all the way to the porch, and Muromsky did not leave until he had his word of honour to come the very next day (with Alexei Ivanovich too) and have dinner as a friend at Priluchino. Thus an ancient and deep-rooted enmity seemed ready to come to an end because of the timidity of the bob-tailed mare.

Liza ran out to meet Grigory Ivanovich. 'What does this mean, Papa?' she said in surprise, 'why are you limping? Where's your horse? Whose is this droshky?' – 'Now that you won't guess,' Grigory Ivanovich answered her, adding in English 'my dear', and he recounted everything that had happened. Liza could not believe her ears. Without allowing her to come to her senses, Grigory Ivanovich announced that both of the Berestovs would be dining with him the next day. 'What are you saying!' she said, turning pale. 'The Berestovs, father and son! Dining with us tomorrow! No, Papa, as you please, but I won't show myself, not for anything.' – 'What, are you out of your mind?' retorted her father, 'how long have you been so bashful, or are you harbouring hereditary hatred for them, like a Romantic heroine? That's enough, don't play the fool...' – 'No, Papa, not for anything in the world, not for any treasures will I appear before the Berestovs.' Grigory Ivanovich shrugged his shoulders and argued with her no more, for he knew you would get nothing out of her by contradicting, and he went to have a rest after his noteworthy outing.

Lizaveta Grigoryevna went off to her room and summoned Nastya. The two of them spent a long time discussing the next day's visit. What would Alexei think if he recognised his Akulina in the well-brought-up young lady? What opinion would he have of her conduct and principles, of her prudence? On the other hand, Liza very much wanted to see what impression such an unexpected meeting would make on him... Suddenly an idea occurred to her. She immediately conveyed it to Nastya; both rejoiced at it as a godsend, and decided they would definitely carry it out.

The next day at breakfast, Grigory Ivanovich asked his daughter whether she still intended to hide from the Berestovs. 'Papa,' Liza replied, 'I'll receive them if you wish it, but only on condition that however I might appear before them and whatever I might do, you won't scold me and won't give any sign of surprise or displeasure.' – 'Again some kind of mischief!' said Grigory Ivanovich with a laugh. 'Well, all right, all right, I agree, do what you want, my little black-eyed rascal.' With these words he kissed her on the forehead, and Liza ran off to prepare herself.

At exactly two o'clock, a home-made carriage with six horses in harness drove into the yard and rolled around the circle of deep-green turf. Old Berestov climbed up onto the porch with the help of two of Muromsky's liveried footmen. His son arrived immediately after him on horseback and went with him into the dining room, where the table was already laid. Muromsky received his neighbours as affectionately as could be, invited them to inspect the garden and menagerie before dinner, and led them along carefully swept paths, covered with a sprinkling of sand. Old Berestov inwardly regretted the time and labour wasted on such useless whims, but stayed silent out of politeness. His son shared neither the displeasure of the thrifty landowner, nor the raptures of the proud Anglomaniac; he was awaiting with impatience the appearance of the host's daughter, of whom he had heard a great deal, and although his heart, as we know, was already engaged, a young beauty, nonetheless, always had a right to his imagination.

Returning to the drawing-room, the three of them sat down: the old men recalled former times and anecdotes of their army days, while Alexei pondered on what role he should play in the presence of Liza. He decided that cold distraction was in any event the most seemly thing, and following on from this he prepared himself. The door opened, and he turned his head with such indifference, with such proud carelessness, that the heart of the most inveterate coquette would have been bound to quake. Unfortunately, instead of Liza, in came old Miss Jackson, powdered, corseted, with downcast eyes and a little curtsy, and Alexei's splendid military manoeuvre went completely to waste. He had not had time to brace himself once more before the door opened again, and on this occasion in came Liza. Everyone stood up; her father was about to begin introducing the guests, but suddenly he stopped and hurriedly bit his lip… Liza, his dark-complexioned Liza, was powdered to the ears and wearing more kohl than Miss Jackson herself; false ringlets, much lighter than her own hair, were fluffed up like Louis XIV's wig; sleeves *à l'imbécile* stuck out like Madame de Pompadour's[39] farthingales; her waist was pulled in tight like the letter x, and all of her mother's diamonds that had not yet been pawned were shining on her fingers, neck and ears. Alexei could not have recognised his Akulina in this ridiculous and brilliant young lady. His father went up to her hand, and he followed him in disappointment; when he touched her little white fingers, it seemed to him that they were shaking. He had, meanwhile, had time to notice her foot, intentionally displayed and shod with the greatest possible coquetry. This reconciled him somewhat with the remainder of her costume. As regards the powder and kohl, to be honest, in his simplicity of heart he had not noticed them at first glance, and did not suspect them afterwards either. Grigory Ivanovich remembered his promise and tried to give no appearance of surprise; but so amusing did he find his daughter's prank, he could barely contain himself. The prim Englishwoman was in no mood for laughing. She guessed that the powder and kohl had been stolen from her chest of drawers, and a crimson flush of annoyance was breaking through the artificial whiteness of her face. She threw fiery glances at the young mischief-maker, who, postponing all explanations until another time, pretended not to notice them.

They sat down at the table. Alexei continued to play the role of a distracted and pensive sort. Liza behaved with false modesty, spoke through her teeth in a sing-song voice, and only in French. Her father was continually forgetting everything in contemplation of her, not understanding her aim, but finding it all most amusing. The English-woman was furious and remained silent. Ivan Petrovich alone felt at home: he ate enough for two, drank his full measure, laughed at his own laughter, and conversed and chuckled more amicably with every passing hour.

Finally they rose from the table; the guests departed, and Grigory Ivanovich gave free rein to his laughter and questions. 'What did you take it into your head to dupe them for?' he asked Liza. 'But do you know what? Powder really does become you; I'm not privy to the secrets of a lady's toilet, but in your place I'd start using powder; not too much, of course, but a little.' Liza was in raptures at the success of her idea. She hugged her father, promised him she would think about his advice, and ran off to mollify the irritated Miss Jackson, who barely agreed to unlock her door to her and hear out her justifications. Liza had felt ashamed to appear before strangers so dark-skinned; she had not dared ask... she had been certain that dear, kind Miss Jackson would forgive her... and so on, and so forth. Miss Jackson, reassured that Liza had not meant to make a laughing stock of her, calmed down, kissed Liza, and, as a token of reconciliation, gave her a jar of English powder, which Liza duly accepted with an expression of sincere gratitude.

The reader will guess that next day, in the morning, Liza did not delay appearing in the grove of their meetings. 'Were you with our master and mistress yesterday, sir?' she said to Alexei at once, 'what did you think of the young lady?' Alexei replied that he had not noticed her. 'That's a pity,' retorted Liza. 'And why's that?' asked Alexei. 'Because I'd like to ask you if it's true what they say...' – 'And what do they say?' – 'Is it true what they say, that I look like the young lady?' – 'What nonsense! Alongside you she's an ugly freak.' – 'Oh sir, it's a sin for you to say it; our young lady's so nice and white, she's so finely dressed! How can I compare with her!' Alexei swore to her that she was better than every possible nice, white young lady, and, to reassure her completely, he began describing her mistress in such funny terms that Liza chuckled heartily. 'However,' she said with a sigh, 'although the mistress may be funny, alongside her I'm still an illiterate fool.' – 'Oh!' said Alexei, 'there's a thing to grieve over! But I'll teach you to read straight away, if you like.' – 'Certainly,' said Liza, 'why not, indeed, have a try?' – 'If you please, my dear; and we may as well begin now.' They sat down. Alexei took a pencil and notebook out of his pocket, and Akulina learnt the alphabet amazingly quickly. Alexei could not contain his admiration of her understanding. The next morning she wanted to try writing as well; the pencil would not obey her at first, but after a few minutes she began drawing the letters quite respectably too. 'What a marvel!' said Alexei. 'Our studies are going quicker than by the Lancaster system.'[40] Indeed, on the third lesson Akulina could already haltingly make out *Natalya the Boyar's Daughter*,[41] interrupting the reading with comments which had Alexei truly astonished, and she scribbled down an entire sheet of aphorisms selected from the same tale.

A week passed, and a correspondence was begun between them. The post office was established in a hollow in an old oak tree. Nastya secretly carried out the duties of the postman. Alexei would bring letters written in a large hand, and there he would find his beloved's scrawls on plain blue paper. Akulina was visibly growing accustomed to a better mode of speech, and her mind was noticeably developing and taking shape.

Meanwhile, the recent acquaintanceship between Ivan Petrovich Berestov and Grigory Ivanovich Muromsky was becoming more and more firmly established, and soon turned into friendship in the following circumstances. Not infrequently did Muromsky think about the fact that, upon Ivan Petrovich's death, the whole of his estate would pass into the hands of Alexei Ivanovich; and in that case Alexei Ivanovich would be one of the wealthiest landowners in the province, and there was no reason for him not to marry Liza. Old Berestov, for his part, although he recognised a certain extravagance of behaviour in his neighbour (or, in his expression, English idiocy), still did not deny that he had many excellent virtues too, for example, rare resourcefulness; Grigory Ivanovich was a close relative of Count Pronsky, a distinguished and powerful man; the Count might be very useful to Alexei, and Muromsky (thought Ivan Petrovich) would probably be glad of the opportunity to marry his daughter off advantageously. The old men thought all this over, each to himself, until finally they discussed it with one another too, they embraced, promised to work the matter out properly, and set about arranging it, each for his own part. One difficulty lay ahead for Muromsky: persuading his Betsy to become more closely acquainted with Alexei, whom she had not seen since the memorable dinner. They did not seem to have liked one another very much; at least, Alexei had not returned to Priluchino any more, and Liza would go off to her room every time Ivan Petrovich favoured them with a visit. But, thought Grigory Ivanovich, if Alexei visits me every day, Betsy will simply have to fall in love with him. It's in the nature of things. Time will settle everything.

Ivan Petrovich was less worried about the success of his intentions. That very evening he summoned his son to his study, lit up a pipe and, after a slight pause, said: 'How is it, Alyosha, that you've said nothing about military service for such a long time? Does a hussar's tunic no longer attract you?...' – 'No, Father,' Alexei replied deferentially, 'I can see you don't wish me to join the hussars; it's my duty to obey you.' – 'Good,' replied Ivan Petrovich, 'I see you're an obedient son; that's a comfort to me; and I don't want to impose on you either; I won't compel you to enter... not immediately... into civilian service; but in the meantime I intend to get you married.'

'To whom, Father?' asked the astonished Alexei.

'To Lizaveta Grigoryevna Muromskaya,' replied Ivan Petrovich; 'a first-rate bride; isn't that so?'

'Father, I'm not thinking of marriage yet.'

'You're not thinking of it, so I have been, and a great deal too, on your behalf.'

'As you wish, but I don't like Liza Muromskaya at all.'

'You'll get to like her later on. Love comes with time.'

'I don't feel capable of making her happy.'

'Her happiness isn't your concern. What? Is this the way you respect your father's will? Excellent!'

'Whatever you say, but I don't want to get married and I'm not going to.'

'You are going to get married, or else I shall curse you and, as God is Holy, I'll sell the estate and squander the money, and I won't leave you a quarter-kopek piece! I give you three days for reflection, and in the meantime don't you dare let me set eyes on you.'

Alexei knew that if his father got something into his head, then, in Taras Skotinin's[42] phrase, you couldn't knock it out again, not even with a nail; but Alexei took after his father, and it was just as difficult to make him change his mind. He went off to his room and began reflecting on the limits of parental power, on Lizaveta Grigoryevna, on his father's solemn vow to make him a beggar, and finally on Akulina. For the first time he saw clearly that he was passionately in love with her; the romantic idea of marrying a peasant girl and living by his own labours occurred to him, and the more he thought about this decisive action, the more good sense he found in it. The meetings in the grove had been discontinued some time before, owing to the rainy weather. He wrote Akulina a letter in his clearest hand and in the most furious style, advised her of the ruination that threatened them, and straight away offered her his hand. He immediately took the letter off to the post office, the hollow, and went to bed very pleased with himself.

The next day, Alexei, firm in his intention, set off early in the morning to see Muromsky and have a frank talk with him. He hoped to excite his magnanimity and incline him to his side. 'Is Grigory Ivanovich in?' he asked, pulling his horse up in front of the porch of the Priluchino castle. 'No, sir,' replied a servant, 'Grigory Ivanovich was good enough to ride out early this morning.' – 'How annoying!' thought Alexei. 'Is Lizaveta Grigoryevna at least in?' – 'Yes, sir.' And Alexei leapt from his horse, passed the reins into the footman's hands and went in unannounced.

'Everything will be decided,' he thought as he approached the drawing room, 'I'll talk things over with her myself.' He entered… and was rooted to the ground! Liza… no, Akulina, dear, dark-complexioned Akulina, wearing not a sarafan, but a white morning dress, was sitting in front of the window reading his letter; she was so occupied that she had not heard him enter. Alexei could not refrain from a joyous exclamation. Liza gave a start, raised her head, cried out, and meant to run away. He hastened to restrain her. 'Akulina, Akulina!...' Liza tried to free herself from him... *'Mais laissez-moi donc, monsieur; mais êtes-vous fou?'*[43] she kept repeating, turning away. 'Akulina! My darling Akulina!' he kept repeating, kissing her hands. Miss Jackson, a witness to this scene, did not know what to think. At this moment the door opened, and in came Grigory Ivanovich.

'Aha!' said Muromsky, 'you seem to have got the matter completely settled already...'

Readers will spare me the superfluous obligation of describing the denouement.

The End
of The Tales of I.P. Belkin

The History of the Village
of Goryukhino

If God sends me readers, then perhaps it will be of interest to them to learn how it was that I resolved upon writing *The History of the Village of Goryukhino*. For that I must enter into certain preliminary details.

I was born of honest and noble parents in the village of Goryukhino on 1st April 1801, and I received my initial education from our sexton. It is to this estimable man that I owe the inclination for reading and literary pursuits in general which developed in me subsequently. Although my progress was slow, it was solid, for in my tenth year I already knew almost everything that has remained to this day in my memory, which is weak by nature, and which, by reason of my equally weak health, I have not been permitted to overburden.

The profession of a man of letters always seemed to me the most enviable. My parents, estimable, but simple people, brought up in the old ways, never read anything, and apart from the ABC which they bought for me, calendars and *The Latest Letter-Writer*, no books were to be found at all. Reading the letter-writer was for a long time my favourite exercise. I knew it by heart and, in spite of that, I found in it new, unnoticed beauties every day. After General Plemyannikov, whose father had once been an adjutant, Kurganov[44] seemed to me the greatest of men. I questioned everyone about him and, unfortunately, nobody could satisfy my curiosity, nobody had known him personally, and to all my questions I only got the answer that Kurganov had written *The Latest Letter-Writer*, which I knew very well already. A shroud of mystery surrounded him like some ancient demigod; sometimes I even doubted the truth of his existence. His name seemed to me fictitious, and the legend about him a hollow myth, awaiting the discoveries of a new Niebuhr.[45] However, he continued to haunt my imagination, and I tried to attach some image to this mysterious figure, finally deciding that he must have looked like the district magistrate Koryuchkin, a little old man with a red nose and sparkling eyes.

In 1812 I was taken to Moscow and put into Karl Ivanovich Meyer's boarding school – where I stayed no more than three months, for we were dismissed before the advance of the enemy, and I returned to the countryside. Upon the expulsion of the two and ten languages,[46] they wanted to take me to Moscow once more to see whether Karl Ivanovich had returned to his former hearth and home, or otherwise to put me into another school, but I prevailed upon my mother to keep me in the countryside, for my health did not allow me to get out of bed at seven o'clock, as is normally the custom in all boarding schools. Thus I reached the age of sixteen, remaining with my initial education and playing ball with my playmates, the only science in which I had acquired a modicum of knowledge during my stay in the boarding school.

At this time I was given a place as a cadet in the ** infantry regiment, where I was until last year, 18**. My stay in the regiment left me few pleasant impressions apart from my promotion to officer rank and the winning of 245 roubles at a time when all I had left in my pocket was one rouble sixty kopeks. The deaths of my dearest parents compelled me to resign my commission and come back to my patrimony.

This epoch of my life is so important for me that I intend to enlarge upon it, begging the pardon of the gracious reader in advance if I should abuse his indulgent attention.

The day was autumnal and overcast. Arriving at the station from which I was to turn off to Goryukhino, I hired free horses and set off down the country road. Although I am by nature of a quiet disposition, still impatience to see once more the places where I had spent my best years took such a strong hold of me that I continually drove my coachman on, now offering him a tip, now threatening him with blows, and as it was more convenient for me to shove him in the back than to take out and undo my purse, I confess I did strike him two or three times, something I had never done in my life before, as the estate of coachmen, I know not why myself, is particularly dear to me. The coachman drove his troika on, but it seemed to me that, as is the coachman's wont, while cajoling the horses and brandishing his knout, he was pulling on the tugs all the same. – Finally I caught sight of the Goryukhino grove; and ten minutes later I drove into the master's yard. My heart was beating hard – I looked around me with indescribable agitation. I had not seen Goryukhino for eight years. The little birches which had been planted by the fence in my time had grown up and now become tall, branching trees. The yard, which had once been adorned with three regular flowerbeds, between which had run a wide drive, sprinkled with sand, had now been turned into an unmown meadow, on which there was a brown cow grazing. My britzka stopped by the front porch. My man was about to go and open the doors, but they were boarded up, although the shutters were open and the house seemed inhabited. A peasant woman came out of the servants' hut and asked who I wanted. Learning that the master had arrived, she ran into the hut once more, and soon the menials had surrounded me. I was touched to the bottom of my heart, seeing familiar and unfamiliar faces – and exchanging friendly kisses with all of them: my playmates as little boys were already men, and the little girls who had once sat on the floor, ready to run errands, were married women. The men cried. To the women I said without ceremony: 'How you've aged,' and they replied to me with feeling: 'And you, sir, how ugly you've grown.' I was led to the back porch, and out to meet me came my wet-nurse, who embraced me like long-suffering Odysseus[47] with crying and sobbing. People ran off to stoke up the bath-house. The cook, who in idleness had now let his beard grow, volunteered to prepare dinner for me, or supper – for it was already getting dark. The rooms in which the wet-nurse and my late mother's maids had been living were immediately cleared for me, and I found myself in the humble abode of my fathers, falling asleep in that same room in which twenty-three years before I had been born.

About three weeks passed with all kinds of trouble for me – I was busy with magistrates, marshals and every possible provincial official. Finally I came into my inheritance and was put in possession of my patrimony; I relaxed, but soon the boredom of idleness began to torment me. I was not yet acquainted with my good and estimable neighbour **. The activities of farming were completely alien to me. The conversation of my wet-nurse, whom I promoted to housekeeper and stewardess, consisted of a total of fifteen domestic anecdotes which were most curious for me, but which she always recounted identically, so that she became for me another *latest letter-writer*, where I knew which line I would find on which page. And the real good old letter-writer I found in the storeroom, amidst all sorts of junk and in a sorry state. – I brought it out into the light and made to set about reading it, but Kurganov had lost his former charm for me; I read it through one more time and never opened it again.

In this extreme it occurred to me that I might try writing something myself. The gracious reader already knows that I was given a poor boy's education, and that I had not had the opportunity to acquire myself what had once been missed, playing with the peasant boys until the age of sixteen, and then moving from province to province, from quarters to quarters, passing the time with Jews and sutlers, playing on tatty billiard tables and marching in the mud.

What is more, to be an author seemed to me so difficult, so unattainable for us, the uninitiated, that the idea of taking up the pen at first frightened me. Did I dare hope someday to number myself among writers, when even my burning desire to meet one of them had never been fulfilled? But that reminds me of an incident which I intend to recount as proof of my eternal passion for my native literature.

In 1820, when I was still a cadet, I happened to be in St Petersburg on official business. I lived in the city for a week and, despite the fact that I did not have a single acquaintance there, I had an extremely enjoyable time: every day I went quietly to the theatre, to the fourth tier of the gallery. I came to know all of the actors by name, and fell passionately in love with **, who one Sunday played with great art the role of Amalia in the drama *Misanthropy and Repentance*.[48] In the morning, returning from the General Staff building, I normally dropped into a humble little confectioner's and read the literary journals over a cup of chocolate. One day, I was sitting absorbed in a critical article in *The Well-intentioned*;[49] someone in a pea-green greatcoat came up to me and gently pulled *The Hamburg Gazette*[50] news-sheet from under my book. I was so engrossed that I did not even raise my eyes. The stranger ordered himself a steak and sat down opposite me; I kept on reading, and paid him no attention; he meanwhile had lunch, angrily scolded the boy for carelessness, drank half a bottle of wine and left. – There were two young men having lunch there too. 'Do you know who that was?' said one to the other: 'That's B., the author.'[51] – 'The author,' I involuntarily exclaimed, and, leaving the journal unfinished and my cup undrained, I ran to settle up and, without waiting for the change, ran out into the street. Looking in all directions, I caught sight of the pea-green greatcoat in the distance and set off after it down Nevsky Avenue – practically at a run. After taking a few steps, I suddenly felt myself being stopped – I looked around, and a Guards' officer observed to me that I ought not to have pushed him off the pavement, but rather stopped and stood to attention. After this reprimand I became more careful; to my cost, I was continually coming across officers and continually stopping, while the author kept going on ahead away from me. Never in my life had my soldier's greatcoat been so burdensome to me – never in my life had epaulettes seemed to me so enviable; finally, right by the Anichkov Bridge, I caught up with the pea-green greatcoat. 'Permit me to ask,' I said, raising my hand to my forehead, 'are you Mr B., whose splendid articles I had the happiness of reading in the *The Contender in Enlightenment?*'[52] – 'No, sir,' he answered me, 'I'm not an author, but a solicitor; though I am very well acquainted with **; I met him a quarter of an hour ago by the Police Bridge.' Thus my respect for Russian literature cost me 30 kopeks in lost change, a reprimand from a superior and near arrest – and all for nothing.

Despite all the objections of my reason, the audacious idea of becoming a writer was continually coming to mind. Finally, no longer being in a state to resist the bent of nature, I sewed together a thick notebook for myself with the firm intention of filling it with whatever I could. I analysed and evaluated every genre of poetry (for I was not yet even thinking of humble prose), and resolved definitively upon an epic poem drawn from the history of the fatherland. I was not long seeking a hero for myself. I chose Ryurik[53] – and set to work.

I had acquired a certain skill in verse by writing out the notebooks which had been passed from hand to hand among our officers, namely: *The Dangerous Neighbour*,[54] *A Criticism of the Moscow Boulevard*, and of *Presnya Ponds*[55] etc. In spite of this, my poem made slow progress and I gave it up on line three. I thought that the epic genre was not the one for me, and began a tragedy, *Ryurik*. The tragedy failed to get going. I tried turning it into a ballad – but somehow the ballad did not lend itself to me either. Finally inspiration dawned upon me, and I began and successfully completed an inscription to a portrait of Ryurik.

Despite the fact that my inscription was not entirely unworthy of attention, especially as the first work of a youthful rhymer, still I sensed that I was not a born poet and contented myself with that first endeavour. But my creative efforts had so bound me to literary pursuits that

I was no longer able to part with the notebook and inkstand. I wanted to stoop to prose. In the first instance, not wishing to occupy myself with preliminary study, the organisation of the plan, the linking of the parts etc., I conceived the idea of writing independent thoughts, without connection, without any order, in the form in which they began presenting themselves to me. Unfortunately, no thoughts occurred to me – and in two whole days I came up with the following observation alone:

A man who does not obey the laws of reason and is accustomed to following the incitements of passions often loses his way and is subject to belated repentance. – A thought that is, of course, true, but no longer new. Abandoning thoughts, I set about tales, but not knowing, through lack of practice, how to set out a fictional event, I chose the remarkable anecdotes I had heard at one time or another from various persons, and tried to adorn the truth with the liveliness of the account, and sometimes with the flowers of my own imagination too. Composing these tales, I little by little developed my style and schooled myself to express myself correctly, pleasantly and fluently. But soon my supply was exhausted, and I again began searching for an object for my literary activity.

The idea of abandoning trivial and dubious anecdotes for a narrative of true and great events had long been troubling my imagination. Being the judge, observer and prophet of ages and peoples seemed to me the highest level accessible to a writer. But what sort of history could I write with my pitiful level of education, where I would not have been anticipated by highly learned and conscientious men? What sort of history had they not already exhausted? Should I start writing a history of the world – but does the immortal work of the Abbé Millot[56] not exist already? Should I turn to the history of the fatherland? What would I say after Tatischev, Boltin and Golikov?[57] And was I the one to root around in the chronicles and try to get to the concealed meaning of a defunct language, when I could not manage to learn the Slavonic numerals?[58] I thought of a history of a lesser volume, the history, for example, of our provincial capital; but here too, how many obstacles, insuperable for me! The journey into town, the visits to the governor and the archbishop, the request for admission to the archives and monastery storerooms, and so on. The history of our district town would be more convenient for me, but it was not diverting either for the philosopher, or for the pragmatist,[59] and presented little food for eloquence. *** was reclassified as a town in 17**, and the only notable event preserved in its chronicles is the terrible fire which occurred ten years ago and destroyed the market and local government offices.

A chance occurrence resolved my perplexity. A peasant woman hanging out the linen in the attic found an old basket filled with chips of wood, rubbish and books. The whole house knew my inclination for reading. – At the very time I was sitting over my notebook, gnawing my quill and thinking about an attempt at rural homilies, my house-keeper triumphantly dragged the basket into my room, exclaiming joyously: 'Books! Books!' – 'Books!' I repeated in delight, and rushed to the basket. I did, indeed, see a whole pile of books in green and blue paper bindings – it was a collection of old calendars. – This discovery cooled my delight, but I was still glad of the chance find, they were books all the same, and I rewarded the laundress' zeal generously with a silver fifty-kopek piece. Remaining on my own, I started examining my calendars, and soon they had a powerful hold on my attention. They made up an unbroken series of years from 1744 to 1799, i.e. exactly fifty-five years. The blue sheets of paper which are usually bound into calendars were covered in writing in an old-fashioned hand. Casting an eye over these lines, I saw in amazement that they contained not only remarks on the weather and household accounts, but also brief items of historical intelligence concerning the village of Goryukhino too. I immediately set about analysing these precious notes and soon found that they presented a complete history of my native land in the strictest chronological order over the course of almost an entire century. They contained, moreover, an inexhaustible stock of economic, statistical, meteorological and other learned observations. From that time on, the study of these notes was my exclusive occupation – for I saw the opportunity to extract from them a narrative that was well-ordered, curious and instructive. – Having become sufficiently acquainted with these precious memorials, I started searching for new sources for the history of Goryukhino. – And soon the abundance of the same amazed me. Having dedicated six whole months to preliminary study, I finally got down to my long-desired labour – and, with God's help, completed the same on the 3rd day of this November in the year 1827.

Now, like a certain historian similar to me whose name I cannot recall,[60] on concluding my arduous feat, I set down my quill and go with sadness into my garden to reflect on what I have accomplished. It seems to me too, that, having written *The History of Goryukhino*, I am no longer needed by the world, that my duty has been discharged and the time has come for me to go to my rest!

Here I append a list of the sources which have served me in the compilation of *The History of Goryukhino*:

1. A collection of ancient calendars. *54 parts.*[61] The first 20 parts are covered in writing in an old-fashioned hand with titlos.[62] This chronicle was composed by my great-grandfather, Andrei Stepanovich Belkin. It is notable for clarity and brevity of style: for example: 4th May. Snow. Trishka beaten for rudeness. 6th – the brown cow died. Senka beaten for drunkenness. 8th – clear weather. 9th – rain and snow. Trishka beaten because of the weather. 11th – clear weather. Newly fallen snow. Hunted 3 hares down, and the like, without any reflection… – The remaining 35 parts are written in various hands, for the most part in the so-called *shopkeeper's*, with titlos and without titlos, generally prolifically, incoherently, and with no observation of correct orthography. In places a female hand is noticeable. Included in this section are the notes of my grandfather, Ivan Andreyevich Belkin, and my grandmother, his spouse, Yevpraksia Alexeyevna – and also the notes of the steward Gorbovitsky.
2. The chronicle of the Goryukhino sexton. I found this curious manuscript in the possession of my priest, who is married to the chronicler's daughter. The first sheets had been ripped out and used by the priest's children for making so-called kites. One such came down in the middle of my yard. I picked it up and was meaning to return it to the children when I noticed that it was covered in writing.

From the first lines I saw that the kite was formed from a chronicle, and, fortunately, I was able to save the remainder. This chronicle, which I acquired for a quarter of oats, is notable for profundity and uncommon magniloquence.

3. Oral legends. – I did not disregard any items of intelligence. But I am obliged in particular to Agrafena Trifonova, the mother of Avdei the headman, who was (they say) the mistress of the steward Gorbovitsky.

4. Census lists, with the remarks of former headmen (accounts and housekeeping books) concerning the morals and the condition of the peasants.

The country known by the name of its capital, Goryukhino, occupies more than 240 *desyatins*[63] of the globe. The number of inhabitants extends to sixty-three souls. To the north it borders upon the villages of Deriukhovo and Perkukhovo, whose residents are poor, skinny and stunted, while their proud owners are devoted to the bellicose exercise of hare-hunting. To the south the river Sivka separates it from the domains of the Karachevo free husbandmen – restless neighbours, well known for the violent cruelty of their ways. To the west it is enveloped by the flourishing fields of Zakharino, prospering under the authority of wise and enlightened landowners. To the east it borders upon wild, uninhabited parts, an impassable marsh, where cranberries alone can grow, where only the monotonous croaking of frogs is to be heard and where superstitious legend supposes there to be the dwelling-place of some demon.

NB. This marsh is actually called *Demon's Marsh*. The story goes that a half-mad farmgirl was apparently watching over her herd of pigs not far from this isolated spot. She became pregnant and was quite unable to give a satisfactory explanation of this occurrence. The voice of the people accused the marsh demon – but this fairytale is unworthy of the attention of an historian, and after Niebuhr it would be unforgivable to believe it.

From the earliest times Goryukhino was famed for its fertility and favourable climate. Rye, oats, barley and buckwheat thrive in its rich fields. A birch grove and a fir forest provide the inhabitants with trees and fallen branches for the construction and heating of their dwellings. There is no shortage of nuts, cranberries, red whortleberries and bilberries. Mushrooms grow in unusual quantities; fried in sour cream, they are a pleasant, albeit unhealthy food. The pond is full of crucians, while in the River Sivka there are pike and burbot.

The inhabitants of Goryukhino are, for the most part, of average height, and are strong and manly in build, their eyes are grey, their hair is light brown or ginger. The women are notable for their noses, which are somewhat upturned, their prominent cheekbones and their rotundity. – NB. *A strapping wench*, this expression is encountered frequently in the headman's notes to the Census lists. – The men are well-behaved, hard-working (especially on their own ploughland), courageous, bellicose: many of them hunt bear single-handed and are famed in the area as fist-fighters; all generally are inclined to the sensual enjoyment of drunkenness. Over and above housework, the women share with the men in a large part of their labours; and they concede nothing to them in bravery, rare is the woman who fears the headman. They make up a powerful public guard, keeping an indefatigable vigil in the master's yard, and are called *spearwomen* (from the Slovene word *spear*). The chief duty of the spearwomen is to beat a stone as often as possible against a sheet of cast iron and thus inspire fear in wrongdoers. They are just as chaste as they are beautiful; to the assaults of the insolent they reply sternly and expressively.

The Goryukhino dwellers have from time immemorial been engaged in an abundant trade in bast, bast baskets and bast shoes. This is facilitated by the River Sivka, which they cross in the spring in dug-out canoes, like the ancient Scandinavians, while at other times of the year they wade across, having first rolled their trousers up to their knees.

The Goryukhino language is definitely a branch of Slavonic, but differs from it just as much as does Russian. It is full of abbreviations and truncations – some letters have been completely obliterated from it or substituted with others. However, it is easy for a Great Russian to understand a native of Goryukhino and vice versa.

When in their thirteenth year, the men would normally marry twenty-year-old girls. The wives would beat their husbands over the course of four or five years. After which, the husbands would start beating their wives; and in this way both sexes had their period of power and a balance was observed.

The funeral rite took place in the following manner. On the very day of death the deceased was removed to the graveyard – so that the dead person should not take up any space unnecessarily in the hut. Because of this it sometimes happened that, to the indescribable joy of relatives, a corpse would sneeze or yawn at the very moment it was being carried out of the village in the coffin. Wives would mourn their husbands, wailing and crying repeatedly: 'Light of my life, brave fellow of mine! Who have you abandoned me to? How am I to remember you?' On returning from the graveyard, they would begin a funeral feast in honour of the deceased, and relatives and friends would be drunk for two or three days, or even for a whole week, depending on their zeal and attachment to his memory. These ancient rites have been preserved even up to the present.

The clothing of the men of Goryukhino consisted of a shirt worn over trousers, which is a distinguishing feature of their Slavic descent. In winter they wore a sheepskin coat, but more for show than out of genuine need – for they normally had the coat thrown over one shoulder, and tossed it off at the slightest job demanding movement.

The sciences, arts and poetry were in quite a flourishing state in Goryukhino from the earliest times. There were always scholars there besides the priest and junior deacons. The chronicles refer to the clerk Terenty, who lived around 1767, and who could write not only with his right, but also with his left hand. This extraordinary man was famed in the area for composing all kinds of letters, petitions, personal passports etc. Having suffered on numerous occasions for his art, obligingness and participation in various remarkable incidents, he died at a great old age, at the very time when he was training himself to write with his right foot, for the handwriting of both of his hands was already too well-known. As the reader will see below, he plays an important role in the history of Goryukhino.

Music was always the favourite art of the educated people of Goryukhino; the balalaika and bagpipes, the delight of tender hearts, can be heard in their dwellings up to the present, especially in the ancient public building adorned with a fir tree and a representation of a two-headed eagle.[64]

Poetry once flourished in ancient Goryukhino. The poems of Arkhip the Bald are preserved to this day in posterity's memory.

In tenderness they would not be inferior to the eclogues of the famous Virgil,[65] in beauty of imagination they are far superior to the idylls of Mr Sumarokov.[66] And although in flamboyancy of style they are inferior to the latest works of our Muses, they are still their equal in ingenuity and wit.

We shall cite as an example this satirical poem:

Straight into the master's yard
Went the headman bold Anton, (2)
And his tallies with him took, (2)
Placed them in the master's hand,
So the master takes a look,
And he cannot understand.
Oh dear, headman bold Anton,
Now you've scarred the master's life,
And you've ruined all the land
With those gifts you gave your wife.

Having thus acquainted my reader with the ethnographic and statistical condition of Goryukhino and with the manners and customs of its inhabitants, we shall now get down to the narrative itself.

LEGENDARY TIMES

Headman Trifon

The form of government in Goryukhino has changed several times. It has been by turns under the authority of elders chosen by the village community, stewards appointed by the landowner, and, finally, under the direct control of the landowners themselves. I shall enlarge upon the advantages and disadvantages of these various forms of government in the course of my narrative.

The foundation of Goryukhino and the original settlement of the same are shrouded in mystery. Obscure legends say that at one time Goryukhino was a wealthy and extensive village, that all of its residents were prosperous, that quit-rent was collected once a year and sent off in several wagons to a person unknown. At that time, everything was bought cheaply and sold at a high price. There were no stewards, headmen did no one any harm, the inhabitants did little work, yet were living in clover, and shepherds watched over their flocks wearing boots. We ought not to be deluded by this enchanting picture. The idea of a golden age is common to all races and only proves that people are never content with the present and, from experience having little hope for the future, they adorn the irretrievable past with all the flowers of their imagination. Here is what is trustworthy:

From the earliest times the village of Goryukhino belonged to the renowned family of the Belkins. But, owning many other patrimonial estates, my ancestors paid no attention to this remote land. Goryukhino paid small tribute and was administered by elders elected by the people at an assembly known as the community gathering.

But over the course of time, the patrimonial domains of the Belkins were divided up and went into decline. The impoverished grandsons of a wealthy grandfather could not give up their luxurious habits – and they demanded the full former income from an estate which had already decreased in size tenfold. Terrible injunctions came one after another. The headman would read them at the assembly; the elders orated, the community grew agitated – and the masters, instead of a doubled quit-rent, received sly excuses and meek complaints, written on soiled paper and sealed with a half-kopek piece.

A gloomy storm-cloud was hanging over Goryukhino, and no one was even remotely aware of it. In the final year of the rule of Trifon, the last headman to be elected by the people, on the very day of the church's patronal festival, when all the people were noisily surrounding the entertainment building (called, in common parlance, the tavern) or wandering through the streets, embracing one another and loudly singing the songs of Arkhip the Bald, a wickerwork covered britzka drove into the village drawn by a pair of nags that were barely alive; on the box sat a ragged Jew – and poking out of the britzka was a head in a peaked cap, which seemed to be watching the people enjoying themselves with curiosity. The residents greeted the carriage with laughter and rude gibes. (NB. Rolling up the hems of their outer garments, the madmen made fun of the Jewish coachman and laughingly exclaimed: 'Yid, Yid, eat a pig's ear!…' *Chronicle of the Goryukhino Sexton.*) But how they were amazed when the britzka stopped in the midst of the village and, jumping out of it, the newcomer in an imperious voice demanded Trifon the headman. This dignitary was to be found in the entertainment building, from which two elders led him deferentially by the arms. – Looking at him menacingly, the stranger handed him a letter and ordered him to read the same immediately. Goryukhino headmen were in the habit of never reading anything themselves. The headman was illiterate. The clerk Avdei was sent for. He was found not far away, asleep under a fence in an alley – and was brought to the stranger. But when he had been brought, either because of the sudden fright, or because of a mournful presentiment, the characters of the distinctly written letter seemed to him blurred – and he was in no condition to make them out. – With terrible curses, the stranger sent Trifon the headman and the clerk Avdei away to sleep, postponed the reading of the letter until the following day and went to the village office, to which the Jew also followed him, carrying his little suitcase.

The people of Goryukhino watched this extraordinary occurrence in speechless amazement, but soon the britzka, the Jew and the stranger were forgotten. The day ended noisily and merrily – and Goryukhino fell asleep, not foreseeing what awaited it.

With the rising of the morning sun, the residents were awoken by knocking at their windows and the call to the community gathering. One after another, citizens appeared in the yard of the village office, which served as the assembly square. Their eyes were dull and red, their faces swollen; yawning and scratching themselves, they looked at the man in the peaked cap and the old blue caftan standing self-importantly on the porch of the village office – and tried to recollect his features, which they had seen at some time. The headman Trifon and the clerk Avdei stood beside him hatless, with an air of servility and profound sorrow. 'Is everyone here?' asked the stranger. 'Is everyone here, then?' repeated the headman. 'Everyone,' the citizens replied. Then the headman announced that an official document had been received from the master, and he ordered the clerk to read it for the community to hear. Avdei stepped forward and read out loud the following: (NB. 'I copied this portentous document at Trifon the headman's, and it was kept there in an icon-case together with other memorials of his rule over Goryukhino.' I myself could not find this curious letter.)

Trifon Ivanov!

The bearer of this letter, my attorney **, is coming to my patrimony, the village of Goryukhino, to enter into the administration of the same. Immediately upon his arrival, gather the men together and announce to them my will as master, namely: They, the men, are to obey the orders of my attorney ** as my own. And all that he might demand they are to carry out unquestioningly, otherwise he ** is to treat them with all possible severity. I have been forced into this by their brazen disobedience and, Trifon Ivanov, by your knavish indulgence.

Signed NN.

Then, spreading his legs apart like the letter X and with his hands on his hips like the Greek Φ, ** made the following brief and expressive speech: 'Now just you look here, don't try and be clever – I know you're a spoilt lot, but I reckon I'll knock the nonsense out of your heads quicker than yesterday's inebriation.' Not in a single head was there inebriation any longer. As if thunderstruck, the men of Goryukhino hung their heads – and dispersed in horror to their homes.

The Government of the Steward **

** took up the reins of government and set about the execution of his political system; it is deserving of particular scrutiny.

Its main foundation was the following axiom: The richer a peasant is, the more spoilt he is – the poorer, the more submissive. In consequence of this, ** strove for the patrimony's submissiveness as the peasant's chief virtue. He demanded a list of the peasants and divided them into rich and poor. 1) Arrears were shared out between the prosperous peasants and exacted from them with all possible severity. – 2) Penurious and work-shy idlers were immediately set to work on the ploughland – and if by his calculation their labour proved inadequate, he would let the other peasants employ them as labourers, for which the former paid him a voluntary tribute, while the ones given into bond slavery were fully entitled to buy themselves out, paying double the annual quit-rent on top of arrears. All sorts of communal obligation fell on the prosperous peasants. And recruiting time was a celebration for the mercenary ruler; for all the rich peasants in turn bought themselves out of it, until the choice finally fell on a scoundrel or on someone who was destitute.[†] Community gatherings were done away with. – He collected quit-rent little by little and all year round. On top of that, he began unexpected collections. The peasants do not really seem to have paid too much more than previously, but they were quite unable either to earn, or to amass enough money. In three years Goryukhino was reduced to utter penury.

Goryukhino became gloomy, the market was deserted, the songs of Arkhip the Bald fell silent. The little kiddies started begging. Half

[†] The accursed steward put Anton Timofeyev in irons – and old Timofei bought his son out for one hundred roubles; while the steward put Petrushka Yeremeyev in chains, and he was bought out by his father for sixty-eight roubles – and the devil wanted to fetter Lyokha Tarasov, but he fled into the forest – and the steward was greatly grieved by this and raged in his words – and Vanka the drunkard was taken away to town and handed over as a recruit. (Report of Goryukhino peasants)

of the peasants were on the ploughland, and the other half were labourers; and the day of the church's patronal festival became, in the expression of one chronicler, not a day of gladness and rejoicing, but an anniversary of sorrow and mournful remembrance.

A Fragment

In spite of the great advantages which are enjoyed by poets (to be honest, apart from the right to use the accusative instead of the genitive case after the particle *not* and some other instances of so-called poetic licence, we do not know of any particular advantages had by poets) – be that as it may, in spite of their various possible advantages, these people are subject to big disadvantages and unpleasantness. I am not speaking of their usual civic insignificance and poverty, which has become proverbial, about the envy and slander of their brothers, of which they become the victims if they are famed, about the contempt and mockery that fall upon them from all sides if their works are not liked – but what would seem to compare with the misfortune that is unavoidable for them; we mean the judgements of fools? And yet even that woe, however great it might be, is still not the extreme for them. The most bitter, the most unendurable evil for a poet is his title, the sobriquet with which he is branded and which never leaves him. – The public look upon him as their property, consider themselves within their rights to demand he give an account of his slightest step. In their opinion he was born for their pleasure and only breathes in order to pick out rhymes. If circumstances demand his presence in the country, the first person he meets on his return asks him: have you brought us anything new? If he appears in the army to look up his friends and relations – the public is sure to demand of him an epic poem on the latest victory, and the newspapermen ask angrily why he keeps people waiting for him so long. If he should fall into thought about his disordered affairs, about a family plan, about the illness of someone dear to him – a vulgar smile immediately accompanies a vulgar exclamation: you're probably so good as to be composing something. – If he should fall in love – his belle buys herself an album specially and is already awaiting elegies. Should he visit a neighbour to talk about some business or simply as a diversion from his labours – the neighbour calls his little son and makes the boy recite the poetry of *such-and-such*, and in the most pitiful voice the boy treats the poet to the latter's own mutilated verse. And this is even called triumph. So what must adversity be like? I don't know, but the latter would seem to be easier to bear. At least, one of my friends, a well-known poet, admitted that these greetings, questions, albums and boys so maddened him that he was continually obliged to restrain himself from some rude remark and to repeat to himself that these good people probably did not intend to make him lose his patience…

My friend was the simplest and most ordinary man, albeit a poet. Whenever that rubbish (that is what he called inspiration) came upon him, he would lock himself in his room and write in bed from morning until late in the evening, would dress hastily to have dinner in a restaurant, would go out for three hours or so, and, returning, would again go to bed and write until cockcrow. He would continue like this for two or three weeks, at most for a month, and it would happen once a year, always in the autumn. My friend assured me it was only then that he knew true happiness. For the rest of the year he would be taking it easy, reading little and not writing anything, and continually hearing the inevitable question: will you favour us soon with a new work of your pen? The most estimable public would have waited a long time for favours from my friend if booksellers had not paid him quite well for his verse. Being continually in need of money, my friend would publish his writings and then have the pleasure of reading judgements on them in print (see above), something he called in his energetic common parlance – eavesdropping by the tavern on what the lackeys are saying about us.

My friend was descended from one of our most ancient noble families, and he was vain about it in the most good-natured way possible. He set just as much store by the three lines of the chronicler in which there was a reference to his ancestors as a fashionable Gentleman of the Bedchamber does by the three stars of his first cousin once removed. Being poor, like almost all of our old gentry, he would tilt his nose up and assert that he would never marry, or else would take for himself a princess of Ryurik's blood, specifically one of the Yeletskaya princesses, whose fathers and brothers, as is well known, do the ploughing themselves nowadays and, meeting one another in their furrows, give their ploughs a shake and say: 'God be with you, Prince Antip Kuzmich, and how much has your princely health ploughed today?' – 'Thank you, Prince Yerema Avdeyevich…' – Apart from this minor weakness, which, incidentally, we ascribe to a desire to imitate Lord Byron, who also sold his verse very profitably, my friend was *un homme tout rond*, a completely round man, as the French say, *homo quadratus,* a quadrilateral man, to use the Latin expression – in our language, a very good man.

He did not like the company of his literary brothers, except for a very, very few. He found in them too many pretensions, with some to sharpness of mind, with others to fervency of imagination, with still others to sensitivity, with yet others to melancholy, disenchantment, profundity, philanthropy, misanthropy, irony and so on, and so forth. Some seemed to him boring in their stupidity, others unbearable in their tone, still others vile in their baseness, yet others dangerous in their double trade – and generally too self-important and concerned exclusively with themselves and their writings. He preferred the company of women and society people to them, for the former, seeing him daily, would cease to stand on ceremony with him and spared him from conversations about literature and the well-known question: have you written anything new?

We have enlarged upon our friend for two reasons: firstly, because he is the only man of letters with whom we have managed to become closely acquainted, and secondly, because we heard the tale presented to the reader today from him.

This fragment probably comprised the foreword to a tale which was not written or was lost. – We did not want to destroy it…

NOTES

1. From Act IV, Scene viii of the comedy of 1782 by Denis Ivanovich Fonvizin (1745–92).

2. The serf's obligation to work for his owner without payment.

3. From the Romantic narrative poem *The Ball* (1828) by Yevgeny Abramovich Baratynsky (1800–44).

4. From the short story of 1823 by Alexander Alexandrovich Bestuzhev (1797–1837), who became, while in exile for his role in the Decembrist rising of 1825, one of the most popular writers of fiction in Russia under the pseudonym 'Alexander Marlinsky'.

5. By bending down the corners of cards punters could double and redouble the stakes.

6. 'Forage-cap' (French).

7. Alexander Petrovich Burtsov (d.1813) was a fast-living hussar who figured in three poems of 1804 by the Anacreontic poet and hero of the Napoleonic Wars Denis Vasilyevich Davydov (1784–1839).

8. In the first edition there followed a sentence which was not to appear thereafter: 'Finally I resolved to go to bed as early as possible and to have dinner as late as possible; thus I shortened the evening and added to the duration of the days, and I saw that it was good.' It is possible that the Biblical language of the final phrase may have prompted the censors to ask for the cut.

9. Alexandros Ypsilantis (1792–1828) was a leading Phanariot Greek who fought in the Russian army in the Napoleonic Wars and in 1820 became President of the Filiki Eteria, or Society of Friends, a secret Greek organisation seeking to overthrow Ottoman rule in Greece. Skouliani was one of a series of battles in an unsuccessful campaign in Moldavia and Wallachia, when on 17 June 1821 a small rebel force was overwhelmed by vastly superior Ottoman numbers on the bank of the river Prut. The battle was described by Pushkin in detail in the short story 'Kirdzhali' (1834).

10. From the ballad of 1813 'Svetlana' by Vasily Andreyevich Zhukovsky (1783–1852).

11. The reference is to the Napoleonic invasion of Russia, begun in June 1812, but for which preparations had begun long before.

12. The inconclusive bloody battle was fought 100 kilometres west of Moscow on 26th August 1812.

13. The inconsolable Queen of Caria (reigned 352–350 BC), who erected a magnificent tomb in Halicarnassus in honour of her late brother and husband Mausolus, and every day until her death allegedly drank wine mixed with his ashes. The tomb was one of the seven wonders of the ancient world and gave rise to the word 'mausoleum'.

14. 'Long Live Henry IV' (French), couplets taken from the comedy of 1774, *Henry IV's Hunting Party* by Charles Collé (1709–83), which became particularly popular in France during the Restoration.

15. The comic opera *Joconde, or the Seeker of Adventures* (1814) by Nicolo Isouard (1775–1818) was a great success in occupied Paris that year.

16. The Russian Emperor Alexander I (1777–1825) was, after Napoleon's retreat to Paris in 1814, the most powerful of all continental rulers.

17. From Act II, Scene v of the verse comedy *Woe from Wit* (1825) by Alexander Sergeyevich Griboyedov (1795–1829).

18. 'And if this be not love, what is it then?' (Italian), the opening words of Sonnet 88 by Petrarch (1304–74).

19. The reference is to the novel in letters *Julie, or the New Heloise* (1761) by Jean-Jacques Rousseau (1712–78).

20. From the ode of 1794, 'The Waterfall', by Gavrila Romanovich Derzhavin (1743–1816).

21. Shakespeare's gravedigger appears in Act V of *Hamlet*; Scott's is in Chapter 24 of *The Bride of Lammermoor* (1819).

22. The retired postman Onufrich in the tale 'The Poppy-seed Cake Seller from Lafertovo' (1825) by Antony Pogorelsky, the pseudonym of Alexei Alexeyevich Perovsky (1787–1836).

23. A line from the poem 'Pakhomovna the Simpleton' by Alexander Yefimovich Izmailov (1779–1831).

24. 'Of our clients' (German).

25. An adapted couplet from Act III, Scene vi of the comedy *The Braggart* (1786) by Yakov Borisovich Knyazhnin (1740?–91).

26. An adapted line from the poem of 1825 'The Station' by Pyotr Andreyevich Vyazemsky (1792–1878).

27. The forests around Murom were notorious for the bands of robbers lurking in them over the centuries.

28. This was the lowest class of civil servant in the Table of Ranks established by Peter the Great.

29. Pushkin scholarship has yet to identify a source for these words.

30. A servant in the poem of 1791 'Caricature' by Ivan Ivanovich Dmitriyev (1760–1837).

31. From the verse tale *Dushenka* (1783), a Russified version of the classical story of the marriage of Psyche (Dushenka) and Cupid by Ippolit Fyodorovich Bogdanovich (1743–1803).

32. From the satire 'Molière!' (1808) by Prince Alexander Alexandrovich Shakhovskoy (1777–1846).

33. A body established in 1763 to deal with the affairs of the Imperial Orphanage in Moscow, it later began to offer loans on the security of estates and serfs.

34. Greek philosopher, grammarian and literary critic of the 4th century BC, whose name has become a byword for a source of harsh and possibly unjust criticism.

35. The pseudonym of the German novelist Johann-Paul Friedrich Richter (1763–1825); the aphorism is from a collection of his thoughts published in Paris in French translation in 1829.

36. 'Our comment remains' (Latin).

37. *Pamela, or Virtue Rewarded*, the epistolary novel of 1740 by Samuel Richardson (1689–1761).

38. 'Calm down, Sbogar, come here' (French). The dog's name comes from the novel *Jean Sbogar* (1818) by French Romantic Charles Nodier (1780–1844) – the eponymous hero is leader of a band of brigands, a latter-day Robin Hood.

39. The Marquise de Pompadour (1720–64), mistress of Louis XV of France.

40. A method of schooling based on a monitorial system devised by Joseph Lancaster (1778–1838).

41. A Sentimental historical tale of 1792 by Nikolai Mikhailovich Karamzin (1766–1826).

42. A character in Fonvizin's *The Minor* – see note 1.

43. 'Let me go now, sir; are you mad?'

44. Nikolai Gavrilovich Kurganov (1726–96) published the first edition of his book, which included information on Russian grammar, proverbs, sayings, anecdotes, poems and encyclopaedic material as well as standard forms of letters, in 1769, after which it was reissued many times.

45. Barthold Georg Niebuhr (1776–1831), German historian, particularly noted for his work on Roman history.

46. A term used for Napoleon's army during its invasion of Russia on the basis of the wide range of nationalities found among its soldiers – Germans, Poles, Italians, Spaniards, Portuguese and Croats, for example, as well as Frenchmen.

47. In Homer's *Odyssey*, the first person to recognise the hero after his twenty-year absence from home is his old nurse Eurykleia.

48. A play of 1789 by the German dramatist August von Kotzebue (1761–1819) – the role in question is that of a young girl, played by students from the theatre school.

49. A journal published in St Petersburg between 1818 and 1826 by Alexander Izmailov – see note 23.

50. One of the oldest of German newspapers, its breadth of coverage made it a valuable source of information on foreign news for Russian journalists such as Bulgarin – see note 51. The allusion is to Faddei Venediktovich Bulgarin (1789–1859), popular novelist and conservative journalist, who was Pushkin's most bitter literary enemy. The reference to a 'pea-green coat' alludes to his activities as an agent of the police, for this was a popular term used for detectives.

52. *The Contender in Enlightenment and Charity*, a monthly journal published in St Petersburg from 1818 until 1825.

53. According to the Russian chronicles, in 862 the Slavs in the Russian lands invited foreign princes to come and govern them, and the call was answered by the Varangian Ryurik, who ruled until 879, marking the beginnings of the organised Russian state.

54. A comic narrative poem circulated widely in manuscript, the work of Pushkin's uncle, Vasily Lvovich Pushkin (1767–1830).

55. Anonymous satirical poems circulated in manuscript.

56. Claude-François-Xavier Millot (1726–85), author of *Elements of General History* in 14 volumes.

57. Vasily Nikitich Tatischev (1686–1750), author of *Russian History* (published posthumously 1768–1848); Ivan Nikitich Boltin (1735–92), author of critical notes, published between 1788 and 1794, on histories of Russia by Le Clerc and Scherbatov; and Ivan Ivanovich Golikov (1735–1801), author of *The Acts of Peter the Great* (1778–89). By the 1820s the work of all the historians referred to here was largely out of date.

58. Old and Church Slavonic used letters and titlos (see note 62) to represent numbers.

59. Here, an adherent of historical pragmatism, an approach to history dealing in cause and effect and the drawing of practical lessons from the past.

60. The allusion is to Edward Gibbon (1737–94), author of *The Decline and Fall of the Roman Empire* (1776–88).

61. Pushkin seems to have miscounted: it should be fifty-five.

62. Marks in Church Slavonic script indicating abbreviations and letters being used as numerals.

63. The Russian unit of area is equivalent to just over one hectare.

64. The village tavern – these establishments were farmed out by the State and thus, in accordance with a law of 1767, bore its symbol.

65. Publius Vergilius Maro (70–19 BC), the greatest of Latin poets.

66. Alexander Petrovich Sumarokov (1718–77), a major Russian poet of the Classical period.

BIOGRAPHICAL NOTE

Alexander Sergeyevich Pushkin was born in Moscow in 1799 into an aristocratic but impoverished family. His mother was the granddaughter of Peter the Great's Abyssinian Engineer-General. The young Pushkin was educated in French, but learnt his native Russian from household servants. He attended the Imperial Lyceum at Tsarkoye Selo, and, at the age of fifteen, published his first poem. By the time he had graduated from the Lyceum at the age of eighteen, Pushkin was already an acknowledged force in contemporary literature.

In 1817, Pushkin took up a post in the Ministry of Foreign Affairs at St Petersburg. Here he lived a riotous existence, and became involved with a group of young men who later formed part of the Decembrist uprising of 1825. His writing took on a more seditious flavour, and in 1820 his political poem 'On Liberty' drew the attention of the authorities and led to his banishment from St Petersburg. Pushkin was moved to the south of Russia, where he was to remain for three years, and where he read the work of Byron for the first time. In 1823, Pushkin was moved to Odessa, a more pleasant place of exile, where to some extent he was able to resume his former life. It was here that he began his greatest work *Eugene Onegin* (1823–31). The following year, however, he was again moved – after the interception of some correspondence – this time to his mother's estate in Mikhailovskoye, where he was kept under surveillance.

Despite the unsettled nature of his life in the 1820s, Pushkin continued to write, and his reputation rapidly grew. When Tsar Alexander I was assassinated in 1825, the new Tsar, Nicholas I, recognised Pushkin's great popularity and, in 1826, his exile was finally revoked. He settled in St Petersburg where he met and fell in love with Natalya Nikolayevna Goncharova, a beautiful young aristocrat, whom he married in 1831.

In the early 1830s, Pushkin wrote and published several poems, plays and short stories, including *Boris Godunov*, *Mozart and Salieri* and *The Queen of Spades*. He found, however, that the Tsar's sponsorship, rather than increasing his literary freedom, led to a more severe censorship. Added to this frustration was that of his marriage, which was becoming increasingly unhappy due to Natalya's extravagant tastes and open flirtations. In 1836 a public scandal was caused by her affair with Baron Georges d'Anthès. Pushkin challenged d'Anthès to a duel in defence of his wife's honour. The duel took place in January 1837, and Pushkin was severely wounded. He died two days later.

Hugh Aplin studied Russian at the University of East Anglia and Voronezh State University, and worked at the Universities of Leeds and St Andrews before taking up his current post as Head of Russian at Westminster School, London. His previous translations include Anton Chekhov's *The Story of a Nobody*, Nikolai Gogol's *The Squabble*, Fyodor Dostoevsky's *Poor People*, Leo Tolstoy's *Hadji Murat*, Ivan Turgenev's *Faust*, Mikhail Bulgakov's *The Fatal Eggs*, and Yevgeny Zamyatin's *We*, all published by Hesperus Press.

HESPERUS PRESS CLASSICS

Hesperus Press, as suggested by the Latin motto, is committed to bringing near what is far – far both in space and time. Works written by the greatest authors, and unjustly neglected or simply little known in the English-speaking world, are made accessible through new translations and a completely fresh editorial approach. Through these classic works, the reader is introduced to the greatest writers from all times and all cultures.

For more information on Hesperus Press, please visit our website: **www.hesperuspress.com**

ET REMOTISSIMA PROPE